NA WILLA AND
THE HOUSE IN THE ALLEY

For Paul & Marie Gaudiamo

THE EMMA PRESS

First published in the UK in 2023 by the Emma Press Ltd
Originally published in Indonesia as *Na Willa dan rumah dalam gang*
by POST Press in 2018.

Text © Reda Gaudiamo 2018
Illustrations © Cecillia Hidayat 2018
English-language translation © Ikhda Ayuning Maharsi Degoul
and Kate Wakeling 2023

ISBN 978-1-912915-45-3

A CIP catalogue record of this book is available from the British Library.

Printed and bound in Great Britain by TJ Books Limited, Padstow, Cornw

theemmapress.com
hello@theemmapress.com
Jewellery Quarter, Birmingham, UK

Publication of this book was made possible, in part, with
assistance from the LitRI Translation Funding Program of
the National Book Committee and Ministry of Education
and Culture of the Republic of Indonesia.

Na Willa

AND THE HOUSE
IN THE ALLEY

Stories by Reda Gaudiamo

Illustrated by Cecillia Hidayat

Translated by
Ikhda Ayuning Maharsi Degoul
and Kate Wakeling

Contents

* Cheep!

Just like Pak

I guess Mbok* is right. I do look like Pak.**

My skin stays pale, even if I play outside all afternoon.

My hair just *is* stiff and straight. If I tie it up at night with strips of newspaper and rubber bands… sure, it'll go wavy for an hour or two. But after that brief happy Curly Hair Time, my hair returns to its straight-as-a-broomstick state.

And my eyes… Yep, just like Mbok says, they vanish when I laugh. I have the exact same eyes as Pak.

Pak loves drawing and he'll draw anywhere, anytime. When he sits out on the terrace, he keeps some blank paper and a pen or pencil to hand. When he's smoking, he'll draw whatever pops into his head. I wonder if Pak carries on drawing the whole time he's at work…

When I sit down next to him, Pak always explains his pictures to me, or he'll make up a story from the little sketches he's drawn.

When we're at church, Pak often draws on the weekly newsletter while he listens to the pastor's speech.

Pak will draw on just about anything: on the calendar, on Mak's*** shopping lists, on yesterday's newspaper…

Even on the DINING ROOM WALL.

---

* Mbok – a household assistant
** Pak – dad
*** Mak – mum

At first, Pak just drew on the little bit of wall by the corner of the table. But after a while, his drawings started spreading everywhere. I wonder if it's just our house that has walls covered in drawings by a grown-up.

I've never seen Farida's father or Bud's father or Dul's father draw anything. The walls in their house are white and clean. But Mak says it's alright.

Pak's drawings are A-MAZING.

Mak and I love colouring them in.

They look extra-excellent in colour.

And me, I love drawing too. I can fill the whole of my sketch book with Very Tiny Yellow Chick and Dul and Ida and Bud and Mbok and Mak and Pak and trees and swings…

Like Pak does.

So yes, I guess Mbok is right: I *am* just like Pak.

Souvenirs

It's been a while since Pak last worked on a ship.

Maybe he's grown tired of sailing round the whole time.

Or maybe he just really enjoys staying at home.

At home with me and Mak.

Although that doesn't mean that he's become a stay-at-home dad. He often goes to Jakarta for work. Or to Malang. Usually, he'll be gone for three or four days. One week max. But when he comes back, he brings us souvenirs.

Mostly, the souvenirs he brings back are beautiful picture books, but I can't really understand much of the actual stories because they're all written in English (so I have to wait till Mak or Pak will read them to me). To be honest,

MAK
DAPAT
APA?

* What did you get, Mak?

3

I prefer toys as a present. But Pak's always buying me books, books, books (and more books). I wonder if there are ONLY bookshops in Jakarta. It does seem like there aren't any toyshops…

As for Mak, Pak doesn't bring her postcards, ashtrays or blotting paper with pictures of boats on it anymore. These days he brings Mak bolts of cloth covered in lovely patterns and drawings, so she can turn the fabric into dresses or curtains.

And then the two other things that Pak never forgets to bring home are my absolute favourite sort of powdered milk, plus a tin with the words CORNED BEEF and a picture of a cow smiling a very large smile on the label. These tins are full of minced meat that you can eat straight from the can. Mak usually mixes the meat with eggs to make an omelette, then she serves it all up with warm rice. Or you can also mix up the meat with flour to make little balls that you dip in whisked egg and fry like a cake. DELICIOUS.

The week

Monday.
  Tuesday.
  Wednesday.
  Thursday.

And now it's Friday.
  Day five of school.
  I've already lined up.
  I've already clapped my hands.
  I've already played games and run around and chased my friends.
  I've already sung really a lot of songs.
  I've already cut up some bits of paper. Then glued them down. Then done some colouring in.
  I've already heard Bu Guru* tell us a story, although this doesn't happen every day. And it's only ever one story at a time.

Today is just like always.
  And I want to go home.

If I was at home, I could be listening to the radio with Mak and we could be learning a new song by Lilis Suryani or Ernie Djohan or Tetty Kadi. Or we could be reading the picture book that Mak bought last Sunday after going to church.
  But the bell hasn't rung yet.
  Maybe the teacher's forgotten to ring it.

---

* Bu Guru – 'Mrs Teacher' (a polite way of addressing your teacher)

5

I'd better remind her.

'Bu Guru…'

'Yes, Willa?' Ibu Juwita comes towards me.

She keeps her hands behind her back.

'Did you forget to ring the bell?'

My teacher looks at her watch. 'Well, it's not time to ring the bell, Willa. Not for a long time yet.'

'Not yet? But why is it such a long time, Bu? I reeeeally want to go home soon.'

'I'm afraid you have to be patient. It's a little while until we all go home.'

'EUGH.'

'What's wrong?'

'I just can't wait any longer. I want to play with Farida and Mak and Mbok…'

'Hmmmm, but you can play with your friends here too. Right, Willa?'

'But everyone is busy cutting and sticking, Bu Guru.'

Bu Juwita turns round and follows of the direction of my finger.

Everyone has their head bowed: Asih, Endang, Gatot, Sumi, Eko, Sri and Joko are all looking down, busy with cutting and sticking pictures. They've been doing this for ages and they *still* haven't finished. Why does everything seem to take so long?

'Would you like to do some colouring in?'

I quickly shake my head because I really am DONE with colouring and cutting and sticking.

And I've already washed my hands.

'I want to listen to the radio, Bu… I want to be with Mak. Poor Mak has to listen to the radio all on her own.'

'A ha, but I'm sure you can listen to the radio with Mak when you get home later.'

'But if I go home now, I can listen to the radio even sooner.'

'You can't go home now, Willa. It's not time. Just wait a little while longer.'

EUGH. What exactly is the meaning of *a little while longer*? I want to go home *now*.

'Okay, how about you go outside for a little while and play in the playground?'

Oh! Play on the swings… Do some somersaults…

But I don't want to play on my own.

'Can't I just go home nooooow, Bu Guru?'

'Hmm…'

'I can't wait to read my new book from Mak!'

'A ha! That's it. Books!' Ibu Juwita takes me by the hand and takes me to look at a white wooden bookcase with glass windows, crammed full of books.

'This is my bookcase,' she says, opening it up.

I knew it! I've been peering at this bookcase since my first day at school. Whenever our teacher reads us a story, she takes the book from here.

It is bananas quite how many books she has.

They're all lined up from the smallest to the largest, from the thinnest to the thickest. There are gazillions of them.

'Now, have a look through and see if you can find a book that you want to read or have a look at. OK, Willa?'

I nod my head quickly. Of course there's one I want to look at. And of course I want to read it with the teacher.

You couldn't count how many books my teacher has: there are just too many. Ibu Juwita tells me I can take one out.

But which one? I want the whole lot.

'Can I take two? Um… or three, Bu Guru?'

'Of course you can. But don't forget to put them back in their places when you've finished, alright?'

I choose one with an elephant, a monkey swinging from a tree, a rhino and a giraffe drawn on the cover. *Fairy Tales from the African Jungle.* The pages inside are covered in writing and there aren't many drawings. The other book I choose has a picture of a boy holding what looks like a smoking teapot. *Aladdin and his Magic Lamp.* Interesting: Aladdin's lamp looks just like Mak's teapot at home.

This Aladdin book looks rather like the Ali Baba book with the pictures that pop up when you open it up. On the first page is Aladdin and his mother, with their house in the background. There are trees and a donkey and a cat. When you turn the page, there's Aladdin's uncle and a well and a great big mountain of sand in the background. All of the pictures pop up. I place the book on the table and look at it from the start. It is totally brilliant.

After a while, I've finished some of the stories from Aladdin so I move onto *Fairy Tales from the African Jungle.* There's a story about a giraffe who dreams of having a shorter neck. There's a tiny tree who longs to grow more quickly. There's a crocodile who wants to be friends with a hippopotamus. And there's a monkey who's fed up of living in a forest. Ahhh, there are so many different stories inside. And the drawings are lovely. And funny.

8

I'm so lost in reading these excellent books that I don't even hear Mak arrive.

'Let's go home, Willa.' Mak has already picked up my backpack and water bottle.

'But I haven't finished this book yet.' I point at the teacher's book.

'Do you want to take it home, Willa?' asks the teacher.

I glance at Mak. She is quiet.

'Yes, please. I would love to take it home.'

'Alright then, you may. Please bring it back to me when you've finished reading.'

'When should that be, Bu Guru?'

'Whenever you're finished, Willa. Take your time.'

'Thank you thank you thank you, Bu Guru.' By now I am jumping around. I am happy! Mak also thanks the teacher. She puts the book inside her bag (the one made of calico with the round iron handle at the top) and I climb into the little rattan chair fitted onto the front of her bike.

We're going home.

Come on, Mak… Hurry up. Hurry UP.
I really really want to get home soon.
I really *really* want to read that book.

Saturday

On Saturdays at school, I don't have to learn anything.

We just eat and sing a new song together.

I only have to bring my water bottle and a little napkin.

After coming into the classroom, everyone sits down quietly.

We tie our napkins round our necks.

Then Ibu Juwita – with a bit of help from Mbok Mar, the lady who works in the school canteen – brings in a huge pan, a stack of bowls and some spoons.

All the chairs and the tables are pushed to the corner of the classroom. And they put that big heavy pan on the table there, along with the bowls and spoons.

'What's inside that big pan?' I whisper to Asih.

'I've no idea.'

'Maybe it's es dawet.' I love es dawet.* It's totally yummy, especially if it comes with little pieces of jackfruit. I could easily drink two cups of it.

'I love es dawet,' says Asih, her eyes wide.

But, hold on a minute… maybe it's not es dawet inside that big pan. Because, thinking about it, if that pan was full of es dawet then the *outside* of the pan would be covered in little water droplets because of all the ice inside. And there are no water droplets to be seen. On the contrary, there's steam seeping out from under the lid.

---

* es dawet – a very sweet iced drink made from coconut milk, green rice-flour jelly and palm sugar syrup

BARANGKALI ES DAWeT

AKU SUKA ES dAWeT

* Maybe it's es dawet   * I love es dawet

I decide I'd better ask the teacher.

I get up from my desk and walk over to the big pan.

'Bu Guru...'

'Yes, Willa?'

'What's in the big pan?'

Suddenly I can feel that the whole class has gone still and quiet.

I turn my head to look round and see that all my friends are staring at me with big, big eyes.

Uh? What's wrong? Can't I ask the teacher something?

But Ibu Juwita seems OK with my question. I don't spy any frowns on her forehead. She even lifts the lid off the pan and a burst of heat rises from it, along with some steam.

'I've made a green bean porridge for you and your friends,' says Bu Guru, trying to whisper in my ear.

'Oh! I thought it was es dawet,' I try to whisper back.

Bu Guru giggles and shakes her head.

I've never tried green bean porridge before.

At home, Mak and Mbok often cook green bean soup, sprinkled with celery and leeks then served with rice and potato cakes. I wonder if there'll be potato cakes to eat with this porridge.

I go back to my desk.

Asih nudges me and whispers, 'So what's inside the pan?'

'It's not es dawet.'

It turns out that this porridge is incredibly sweet.

And it doesn't come with potato cakes.

I am, let's say, not a big fan.

But I still love spending Saturdays at school, even if there's no es dawet waiting inside the teacher's big saucepan. Because, as soon as we finish eating, Bu Guru teaches us new songs:

> *Kucingku belang tiga*
> *Sungguh manis rupanya*
> *Meang-meong bunyinya*
> *Tanda lapar perutnya*
>
> *My cat has three stripes*
> *Her face is so sweet*
> *She says meow-meow*
> *which means her tummy's hungry*

Just like my Very Tiny Yellow Chick who says *squawk squawk*.

That is his way of saying GIVE ME FOOD.

Friends

Apparently Asih doesn't like wearing shoes.

She says they make her feet itch. So she wears a pair of pink plastic sandals to school. I want to wear sandals too. But Mak won't let me because she says I'm not allergic to shoes and so there's really no reason at all for me to wear anything other than shoes to school.

I don't understand why Gatot stutters when he speaks. And sometimes what he says just doesn't make sense. Why can't he talk like everybody else? Like me. Like the teacher and like Mak. I never quite know what he's talking about, so I'm always guessing what's on his mind. Doing this makes him really cross.

Then there's Sumi and Sri who have exactly the same faces. They're the same height. And they have the same voice. Mak told me they're twins. They wear the same dresses to school. Sumi often wears a red ribbon and Sri wears a yellow one – Mak says that's how we're supposed to tell the difference. But I already know which one's Sumi and which one's Sri. Sri is always smiling. And Sumi isn't. In fact, she's pretty miserable. Yesterday, when she dropped her pencil and it snapped in two, she started crying in no time at all. Poor Sumi.

Eko loves coloring. But he doesn't like cutting and gluing things down. I don't know why. And I always forget to ask him why.

Our teacher talks to us only in Indonesian. Joko only answers the teacher's questions in Javanese. But the teacher says we all have to speak in Indonesian. Joko nods his head, before he answers 'Ngigih, Bu Guru' (which means 'Yes certainly, teacher' in Javanese).

Oh! And Endang seems to put powder on her face every day. Her face is much paler than her neck and hands. I must say she smells lovely. I'd like to smell just like her.

Gatot

Today I try to have a proper conversation with Gatot.

He doesn't need to do all that stuttering. Right?

So every time he speaks, I whack my hand down on the table. To make him carry on speaking without stopping. He seems a bit surprised. And to be honest, his sentences are quite difficult to understand when I hit the table. And then his face and his ears turn red. His nose wrinkles up. He looks like he might be about to cry.

'Willa, Gatot…' I see that our teacher is suddenly standing beside me.

'I just wanted to help Gatot speak normally, Ibu Guru, and stop fumbling around with his words…'

'I see… So is this why you're hitting the table so hard?'

'Yes, Bu…'

Gatot (with his nose all wrinkled up) says: 'But… but… but.'

'But why?' I finish his sentence for him.

His eyes grow wide. He looks thoroughly unhappy.

But why would he look like that? I was just trying to help him speak a bit more quickly.

'Well, you're very kind, Willa. But I think we can agree that this table-banging is not really the best technique to help,' says the teacher, and she gently rubs Gatot's head. He seems a lot less unhappy than before.

'Let me see, how about I help Gatot with his talking and you go off and play with your other friends. Or you could choose a book from the library? How does something like that sound? A good plan?'

Well that's fine by me.

Face powder

So at last I tell Mak about my friend Endang – the one who uses bedak (that special face powder) every day.

Her face powder smells so good. I've smelt it ever since our first day of school when she held my hand as we went into the classroom.

I thought it was just going to be that one day that Endang used this lovely, fragrant face powder.
  But then the next day she had it on.
  And then the day after that. And the day after *that*.
  I can always tell when she's wearing it because her face looks so pale and soft, even though her neck stays brown, just like her hands and her legs.

Actually, I get to use powder too. After a shower, Mak sprinkles talcum powder on my back so my skin feels all tingly. But my powder doesn't really smell of anything. And if I put too much of it on then I start feeling tingly all over. Maybe that's why Mak never puts it on my face. Or else I'd be sneezing the whole time.

I'm pretty sure Endang's powder is different from the sort I use after washing though. But I think Mak might use the same powder as Endang.

Because yes, Mak has her own powder. And it's different from mine. Mak puts it on whenever she goes to church or to visit Nyonya Chang's office or to go to a party at Ida's house or even just when she goes to the mall.

Mak's powder is in a box with a dancing woman on it, who is wearing red and black dress and holding a red and white lacy fan. The powder is called MAJA. It sits on the table with the mirror on it in Mak's room. Pak brings back this powder for her when he goes to Jakarta.

Mak tells me that only grown-ups should use this sort of powder and that children like me, well, we just use talcum powder. But Endang is a child, just like me, and she wears this grown-up powder to school every day. So I decide that maybe I *can* use a little bit, just like Endang.

I just want to try a teensy tiny little bit. I promise I won't use much.

So, after washing, I creep into Mak's room and open her box of powder. Mmm, it smells so good. I think I like this MAJA powder even more than I like Endang's powder.

I pat the little cotton pad very slowly and carefully on the powder, and then I put the powder on my face, just as I've seen Mak do it. But before I've even got to the bit round my eyes, I start coughing.

Ow. OW. My eyes hurt. Help!

I shriek Mak's name.

'Willa, what's happened?' Mak's already standing behind me.

'The powder, Mak! Quickly! My eyes…'

Mak pulls my hand away from my face.

She uses her handkerchief to wipe my face.

'Go and wash your face and get rid of the rest of it.'

I nod my head. Mak follows me out of the room.

My face feels cold after washing it, but at least my eyes have stopped hurting.

Mak is now cleaning the powder off the top of the table. The box has been put away in the very top drawer at the corner of her dressing table. Even with a stool, I couldn't reach it now.

'So, you wanted to use my face powder?' asks Mak.

I nod. I daren't look at her face because I just know that her eyebrows are going to be all knotted up and joined in the middle.

'Yes, Mak.'

'And why did you do that?' Mak twists my shoulder.

'I wanted to be like Endang.'

'Oh, that Endang!'

I nod. 'Yes! You remember? The one who uses the lovely face powder every day at school... Every. Single. Day.'

'Willa, but the face powder that I use, well, it's only made for adults. For people like me. Or your teacher. It's not to be used by children. It's not good for your skin.'

Yep. I knew this. She'd already told me.

'But what about Endang...'

'Well, for children, you can use talcum powder on your body – that's absolutely fine. After you have a bath or shower then yes, you sprinkle it on your body. It stops you sweating. But you don't need to put it on your face.'

Humph.

'But Endang...'

'You say she uses face powder every day?'

'She does. Every single day. And the powder just smells so good.'

I have this picture in my head: of Endang's super-pale face and then Endang's arms, hands and legs which are super-brown. And when I sit next to her, she smells so good. Not like the 'unscented' talcum powder from the can that I put on every morning and night after a shower.

'Willa, listen to me. This face powder and whatever the one that Endang's been using… well, they're not made for children. You don't need to put that powder on your face. It really isn't necessary. That powder with the perfume is designed for mums and aunts and everyone whose skin isn't very smooth anymore – for people whose skin isn't like child's skin anymore. The older we get, the rougher our skin becomes. So we use this kind of powder to keep our skin smooth. And to encourage us to use it every day, they put some sort of chemical perfume inside the powder. But your skin, Endang's skin… you already have beautiful skin – it's so soft and so smooth. You don't need to do anything at all to your skin.'

'Hmmmm,' I say. 'But…'

'Yes yes yes, I know: Endang uses her mum's face powder every day. But you know what, you don't have to be like Endang.'

Humph. I've *always* wanted to be like Endang. So what should I do?

'Wait, can I ask you a question: if Endang was wearing her clothes inside out, would you do the same thing as her?'

'Oh! No way. I wouldn't put my clothes on like that.'

'Or if Endang ate salak* seeds every day, would you want to eat them too?'

'Eugh. Absolutely NOT.'

'So there we have it. We don't have to follow other people. Especially when the things we're copying aren't very good for us. Understood, Willa?'

The thing is, of *course* if Endang wore her clothes inside out, I wouldn't copy her. As for eating salak seeds, they're totally disgusting so I wouldn't do it. But we're talking about face powder…

Eugh. I wonder why Mak has such a different way of thinking about these things from Endang's mum.

---

* salak – sometimes called 'snake fruit', salak is a tasty fruit with soft white flesh inside but a brown scaly skin that (you guessed it) looks and feels like snake skin. Each segment of the fruit has a large and bitter seed inside it that you definitely *wouldn't* want to eat.

Records

There's a shop in the corner of Siola* which sells records.

The shopkeeper is a man who knows Mak very well.

His name's Pak Johan. When Mak stops by the shop, Pak Johan always welcomes her by playing a new record, hoping that once she's heard it she'll buy it.

But Mak doesn't buy all the records Pak Johan plays her. Sometimes she comes just to explore and listen to some new records. Then she buys them if they're *really* interesting for her. She buys both big and small records.

But only one at a time.

Mak has all sorts of different kinds of records.

If she piled them up, they'd reach as high my knees, for sure.

Gus Salim, Ida's big brother, often borrows one of Mak's favourite records when it's Eid Al-Fitr. When their guests arrive, he plays this record so loudly that me, Mak, Pak and Mbok can pretty much hear the whole thing inside our house too.

There's only one song on this record. Mak loves playing it over and over and over again. She says the lyrics are beautiful. I know this song so well now:

> *Dear humankind*
> *If you're stained*
> *This world is only shadows*
> *For creatures of God's creation*

---

* Siola – the name of a famous department store in Surabaya

Without warning
This world will perish
We will return to the beginning
Facing our One God

The song's called 'The Majesty of God'.

        * Dear humankind...
   * If you're stained...

The windows

Sunday. I still have to wake up early and have a shower.

Today we're going to the church in Jendral Sudirman Street. It's a church with very big tall doors and windows, and huge seats.

After the bell rings three times, the priest goes up on stage, gives a short speech and everyone starts saying, 'Amen, Amen, Amen…'

Then the priest starts talking again.

He sings a song.

We pray.

We sing.

The priest then continues his speech. Which is usually SO LONG and lasts for ages.

We pray again. Also for ages.

Then we sing together again.

When we reach the chorus that goes 'Halleluya, halleluya…' this means it's all pretty much finished.

Then everyone stands up, gets in line and says hello and goodbye to the priest. Standing next to the priest, there's Tante Siok (Pak's friend) who likes giving little pictures with wavy edges (a bit like stamps) to the children. I get one too. Usually she gives just one picture to each child, but ever since I explained to her that Farida longs for them as well, she now gives me two. After we've shaken hands with the priest, everyone heads home. Well, not all of us. Mak, Pak and some of their friends hang about in the church office. They count up all the money from the collection and

I wait for them in the churchyard. Mak says I can also have a snooze on a bench inside, but I mustn't play near the door or windows so I don't trap a finger in the hinges.

This Sunday I don't go and play in the churchyard. It's pouring with rain and there's thunder and lightning to boot. Mak says I'd better stay inside.

But what can I play? I've been messing about on the benches and lying down on them. I've even played underneath them. Just like last Sunday and all the Sundays before. I really want to be home now. But Mak and Pak haven't finished yet and the rain is falling harder and harder.

I walk round the church and stop in front of one of the giant windows. They're wide open and not moving, even though the rain is streaming down them. The windows have metal handles holding them in place. All of them. A HA, not quite. There's one that's missing the handle, so every time the wind blows the window swings back and forth. OK! I decide it'll be very very very very good fun to swing on this window.

So yes, it's true that Mak has told me not to play with the windows and the doors, but I promise myself that I'll be very careful. The windows are so big. The handles are so big. So if I hold on tight, nothing will happen, right? And I won't swing on it for long.

At least, not until Mak catches me.

I just want to try it. Just the once.

I climb up to the window, the one with the missing handle. I put my feet on the bottom of the window frame and I hold onto the round knobs in the middle. I push my feet backwards and forwards, so the window slowly opens and closes.

Then I swing round, from the left to the right.

This is GREAT.

I'm not sure how long I've been doing it but suddenly I hear Mak calling me.

Whoops. I'd better get down quickly, before Mak sees me hanging off this window.

And I don't know why but my feet slip. They're not balanced on the frame anymore. Whoops. I nearly fall off. I try and get into a different position so I can jump down. But... the window closes and it catches my finger in the frame. It's all so fast. My finger is squished.

I shout and cry and scream. My finger is stuck. I don't have a finger anymore. Heeeeeeelp!

Mak runs to me. She holds me tight.

Straightaway she puts my pinched finger in her mouth. She sucks my finger on and on and on. Gradually, it stops hurting.

And I stop crying.

And, of course, I still have all my fingers.

Mak and I go straight home after the accident. Pak stays on at the church.

Mak is angry with me. This I know because she stays silent all the way home.

She doesn't need to say a thing. This is the first time I've ever swung on the church windows. And it'll be the last.

Oom Sie #1

Pak's office is on Johar Street.

Every day he goes to the office early in the morning and comes home in the afternoon.

If he has lots to do, Pak doesn't come home till the evening. Sometimes he even stays OVERNIGHT in the office. And if he has a big deadline, he'll work on Sundays too.

At work, Pak has a good friend called Oom Sie. Mak says Oom Sie has helped Pak so he doesn't need to work on the ships anymore. So he doesn't have to leave home for months and months. So Pak can come home every day now.

Oom Sie is like Farida: he comes to visit us every single day.

Each day he comes with his shiny bicycle.

When the wheels spin, the bike makes a little 'tick… tick… tick' sound. Mak says it's because his bike is so fine and cared-for.

Whenever he visits us, Oom Sie always wears the same clothes: a short-sleeved white shirt, brown trousers and shiny black shoes. He and Pak always drink a cup of coffee and smoke a cigarette.

Oom Sie and Pak have very good conversations and they are always laughing together. Sometimes Mak has a quick conversation with them after she serves the coffee.

But rarely for long, because she's allergic to cigarette smoke.

I don't like it when Mak stays with them for a long time, because then I don't have anyone to listen to the radio with.

I once sat with Pak and Oom Sie on the terrace. I tried to follow the conversation but after a while I went back into the house because I couldn't understand a word of what were they talking about. Mak says it's because Pak and Oom Sie speak in Dutch.

Pak is quite tall and just little bit chubby, whereas Oom Sie is short and skinny. He has a long wrinkled neck. He has a long face and a long nose – and the tip of this long nose curves downward.

Oom Sie's eyes are like Pak's: small and slightly slanted. When you look closely, Oom Sie looks like a man who doesn't have cheeks. Or he *does* have cheeks, but they aren't full like Pak's. Oom Sie has straight hair like Pak, but he lets it grow a bit longer. Pak's hair is short like a brush, but Oom Sie has a fringe that hangs down over his eyebrows so he is always having to push it to the left or to the right. Whenever he's talking, you'll notice some of his hair falling down over his face.

And whenever his hair covers his face, he'll push it behind his ears again. And then he'll carry on speaking and then his hair will flop down AGAIN, so he has to push it to the side, over and over again. I do wonder why he doesn't cut it short, like Pak. Short and comfortable. Surely you need to be able to concentrate on having a conversation without constantly needing to fiddle about with your hair?

Pak and Oom Sie could chat FOREVER.

Once, I was all ready to go to school when I saw Oom Sie on the terrace.

Apparently he hadn't gone home from the night before. Gosh. What did they talk about all night long? I wonder how they managed to stay up all night without sleeping.

On the way to school, I tell Mak I'd like to have a friend like Oom Sie who would stay awake with me all night long. So I could play the whole time without being sleepy and read loads of books. I wouldn't need to go to sleep.

'Willa, when you're grown up and visiting a friend, you have to remember to go home. Especially when night comes. Your friend might like to go to sleep and have a rest too. If it gets late and you can't get home immediately, then you could stay there for the night. But you should avoid staying up all night long. Have you got that, Willa?'

Oh!

'So if Oom Sie comes again tonight, will you tell Pak that it's time to sleep?'

'Oh, Pak will talk to Oom Sie. Oom Sie is Pak's friend. And Pak is a grown up: he can talk to his friend directly.'

A *ha*.

Oom Sie #2

This evening Oom Sie comes to the house again.

He brings his bicycle again.

He wears a short white shirt, brown trousers and black shiny shoes again.

Pak has had his shower and is already out on the terrace, sitting on a wicker chair.

There are cigarettes and lighters on the table. After putting his bike in front of the fence, Oom Sie sits down beside Pak. They begin to chit-chat again. Just like yesterday.

Mbok brings out kue tambang* inside a glass jar with a red paper lid.

Mak follows Mbok.

I follow Mak.

When Mbok goes back to the kitchen, Mak takes a chair and sits down, patting Pak's shoulder. She says: 'Don't forget you're taking Willa to school tomorrow morning, will you? Early in the morning. So, perhaps it's best if you *don't* talk all night and stay up till morning. So, not like yesterday. OK?'

Pak will take me to school tomorrow? I didn't know about this. And why do I need to be accompanied, as if I don't go to school by myself. Sometimes Mak walks me to the corner of the alley, but I go by myself after that.

My question is: does Pak even really know where my school is?

---

* kue tambang – fried twists of dough

'Ah, Pak will be fine, Willa. Let's just get everything you need for tomorrow ready.' This is what Mak says when I tug at her skirt and ask her if I should tell Pak how to get to my school.

Mak stands up from the chair, leaving Pak and Oom Sie out on the terrace.

I follow her again.

Not long afterwards, Pak comes into the house.

Oom Sie has already gone!

Pak sits down in front of our radio which is playing beautiful Javanese songs.

Mak whispers that I should brush my teeth and get ready for bed.

'But Mak... I'm not sleepy yet.'

'That's ok, just try to get to sleep. You'll be wake up earlier tomorrow, because you're going with Pak. You'll have to tell him the way to school. I'm hoping you two aren't going to get lost.'

Oh yes, Pak is taking me to school tomorrow.

Now, if Pak goes down the wrong road, I'll be late for school. And that's unthinkable.

So I go to bed.

Going to school with Pak

It's early in the morning and I'm already up. Mak is too.

I have a shower and put on my white socks and my shoes. But how about Pak? Where is Pak? He's not in the kitchen. Is he already wake? Heck.

Oh, wait a minute... I hear whistling coming from behind the door.

He's just finished a cigarette and is about to eat breakfast.

He has white bread with butter and sugar on top and he drinks hot tea without any sugar. My lunch box (filled with omelette cut into little squares) and my water bottle are already in Pak's hands.

'So, are you ready to show me the way to go to school, Willa?'

I nod.

I hold Pak's hand and we go outside. I explain how we get to school: first we have to turn left, then right, then turn right again, then left again, and then the school is right there.

Mak comes with us to the front of the house. I climb into the seat on the front of the bike. We set off, with Pak pedalling and whistling. I don't know the tune. It seems like a happy song so I bob my head in time. I forget to tell him to turn right because I'm enjoying listening to him so much. But, surprisingly enough, he knows the way to school. When we arrive, he turns his bike round and says goodbye.

'I'll pick you up this afternoon, Willa!' Then he waves and heads off to work.

When the school day is finished, I see that Pak is already in front of the school, waiting for me on his bicycle.

'Willa, look, you have a present from Oom Sie.' Pak gives me a parcel wrapped in brown paper and tied with thick red string.

'You can eat them this evening, or you can put them in your lunchbox tomorrow,' says Pak. When I open the parcel, I find two chocolate bars wrapped in white paper with big blue letters that say VOLLE MELK. There are also some chocolates with swirly patterns and a few more in the shape of umbrellas. Wowee. Oom Sie is an excellent person.

'Pak, can I eat some of these chocolates while we're on the bike?'

Pak is silent for a little while, then he says, 'Sure. But try to not eat all of them, if possible? Share some with Mak, alright?'

This is the best ever journey home: riding on the bike with Pak while eating chocolate. And one chocolate is enough. I decide to eat the rest with Mak when we get home.

On the way back, I tell Pak all about my friends Asih, Eko and Endang (who uses the face powder). I tell him about Joko who speaks only Javanese, Gatot who never finishes his sentences, Sumi who cries whenever she doesn't finish her colouring, and Sri who is always teasing her. By the time I've told all these stories, Pak can't stop laughing.

And while Pak pedals along, just like Mak he loves to sing and make up his own songs. Mak often sings about the flowers in the garden – the roses and jasmine – but Pak makes up a song all about me and my friends.

Willa, oh Willa, in her new school she has so many new friends!
There's Gatot, Sumi, Ekoooo
Asih, Endang, Sriiiii, and Jokoooo!

Ahhhh, I love Pak's song.

Willa, oh Willa, in her new school she has so many new friends!
There's Gatot, Sumi, Ekoooo
Asih, Endang, Sriiiii, and Jokooooo!
And Jokoooooooo!

The rocking horse

In the evenings during the holidays, if I am not too tired, Pak loves taking me and Mak to have fun at THR, a big amusement park in Surabaya. We go there by becak.* It is The Most Wonderful Place on Earth. There are games and performances. There's a windmill. There's a throw-the-ball game with prizes, and we can go and watch ludruk** too… There's so much to do.

But my very favourite thing to do among all this is to ride on this wooden horse that goes up and down and up and down. Mak says this is called a carousel.

When I'm riding on this wooden horse, I have to hold on tight to a metal pole that runs through the horse's body. The floor is metal too and there are lots of horses on the ride. Each one goes up and down, spinning round and rising then falling, up and down. Once I've had a go on one of these horses, I don't want to get off the ride. And I certainly don't want to go home.

Once, Pak went to Jakarta with Oom Sie for an important meeting. He was away for a long long time, but when he got home he had bought me a wooden horse! It was big and strong, just like the one on the carousel at THR. Ah, Pak: I had a hunch there must be a toyshop *somewhere* in Jakarta.

---

* becak – (pronounced be-chak) a little vehicle (sometimes with a motor, sometimes pedalled like a bike) for two or three passengers, which you can hail like a taxi
** ludruk – a type of East Javanese theatre that tells tales of every day life (and is often very funny)

The wooden horse that Pak bought me is mostly black, but its four legs are white. It has a red nose and the saddle is painted bright white. There's a piece of curved wood under the horse's feet so the whole thing rocks back and forth. Mak says that if the rocking horse was just a little bit bigger, she'd like to come and ride it with me.

At first, we put Poni the horse in the living room. Mak said it looked very grand here. But it only lasted for one day, because when I rode it the horse crashed into the table legs, so we had to move it to another part of the house. It wasn't safe, Mak said.

Pak suggested we put it outdoors, but Mak didn't agree because the rain would damage the horse as it isn't waterproof. So, we put Poni in the playroom. Which is where the special swing that Pak made for me (from ship's rope) still hangs.

Ever since Poni arrived, I hardly ever play with the swing. Or rather, I *never* play with the swing. I just love riding Poni too much. After school, after lunch, after a nap, after a shower, after dinner: I just want to play with Poni. I don't have time for anything else. I don't even want to read or to play with Farida, Bud and Dul.

One afternoon, when I'm busy riding on Poni, Mak comes in with Farida, Dul and Bud.

'Your friends were waiting for you outside the house yesterday, Willa. I think it might be nice to let them come and play with you here.' Then she leaves us – that's me, Bud, Ida, Dul and Poni – all together in the big playroom. Farida stands in front of Poni. Her mouth hangs open for a long long time. Her eyes are open wide as well.

'This. Is. Amazing!' she says in a loud voice. Dul doesn't say anything. He's slowly walking round Poni, tapping the horse with his stick. Meanwhile, Bud starts trying to jump up and ride the horse, even though I'm still sitting on it.

'Me! Me! Me! I want to ride it!' he says, snorting some snot through his nose.

'No no NO! Please just wait a minute and give me a chance to get down.' I have to get off the horse immediately, or me, Bud and Poni are all going to fall on top of one another.

By now, Bud has managed to get on the back of Poni and he's moving around and laughing. Soon after that, Farida climbs up there too. And then Dul wants to ride it too but he can't. Instead of riding the horse, he's just falling off it. He can't stand without his walking stick and it's just too complicated for him. Dul looks so miserable. And a moment later he's vanished. Dul has gone home.

The next day, Farida and Bud come and ride the horse again. But it doesn't take long until Farida gets bored. Me too. We get tired of waiting for Bud get down from Poni. At long last, Farida and I start playing dolls and pretending to cook and lying on the floor and reading books aloud. But, unlike us, Bud never tires of riding that wooden horse. He could ride Poni from afternoon to evening. He rocks and rocks all alone in that dark playroom.

One time, Bud even falls off Poni because he falls asleep for a moment. I think to myself: he'll stop riding the wooden horse now that he's fallen off it. But Bud still loves it. That is, until he falls asleep again.

* Bud's run away!

One afternoon after school, Mak takes me shopping at
Siola. We wander round, looking at things and trying to
spot some new plates. When we get back, there's a crowd
in front of our house. Bud's mum is crying and she's
surrounded by other women. What's wrong? Mak goes up
to her to find out what has happened.

'He's gone, Bu Marie! Bud's run away!'

'Bud? He's run away from home?'

'After school, he was already gone. I thought he was
playing with Dul but he wasn't! Oh Buuuuuud…'

'But wait! Perhaps…'

Mak doesn't even finish her sentence. She runs straight
into the house. I follow her. Inside, Mak checks the
playroom where Poni is. We can hear the sound of wood

rocking on the floor: *crack, crack, crack…* and there, of course, is Bud on the top of the wooden horse. Fast asleep.

He must have come into the house when Mak and I had already gone. He'd asked Mbok for permission but she was so busy with tidying and ironing that she'd forgotten he was in the house.

Mak and Mbok wake Bud up and take him outside. In front of the house, Bud's mother and all the other mothers are waiting. Bud's mother is so happy, she claps her hands. Everyone is happy. Bud just grins, then sucks up another bit of his snot.

All the way home, Bud's mum growls at him and pulls at his ears.

'Next time, you have to come home first before you go off playing. And if you plan to go to your friend's house, at least ask me for permission. I thought you'd run away or had an accident with a train. You made me so angry and scared. I won't allow this to happen again, Bud! Got that?'

Bud screams 'Ouch! Ouch! OUCH' and jumps up and down. I wonder if all that ear pulling really does hurt.

From then on, Bud rarely comes to play on the rocking horse. Or if he does, he doesn't stay and play for long. No, instead he makes sure he's home before it's dark.

The pine tree

Do you remember the pine tree in front of our house?

Well, it's not the same as the pine tree they have at church, which is triangle-shaped and crammed with decorations at Christmas. Nope, my pine tree has lots and lots of branches and the branches are on the left and the right, and they're at the front and at the back and EVERYWHERE. The pine needles are soft and they sway gently in the wind. I like pulling off a few needles then pretending to make spice paste with them. I mash them up with the pestle and mortar that Mak bought me from the market. Farida loves pretending to make a spice paste too. She likes stirring it round and round.

Sometimes, Mak cuts one or two branches off the pine tree and puts them in a vase of water. Then she adds some stems of flowers that feel like they're made of paper. Mak says they're called Oleander. This vase of flowers and pine needles always sits on the table in the dining room. After a day, Mak will throw away the flowers because the petals start to go brown and frankly they don't smell all that good. But the branches can stay in the vase for a few days.

One day, Mak takes a saw and cuts a big branch off the pine tree. She puts the branch inside a bucket filled with soil and goat poo (which Farida's mother gave her). Then she waters it every day and every night.

Mak says she hopes the branch will get bigger and bigger and eventually grow into a proper tree. For the first few days, it loses lots of its needles and starts looking a bit dried out and faded, but after a couple more days the branch starts to grow. And now it no longer looks all sleepy and worn out. And there are more and more pine needles. The branch is getting bigger and stronger.

One Sunday, Mak says the branch in the bucket is now strong enough and has grown roots.

'It's time we bring it into the house,' she says.

'Why, Mak?'

'We're going to use it as a Christmas tree.'

OK! So we're going to have a real Christmas tree at home, just like at church.

'Can we decorate it, Mak?'

'Yes! Let's make some decorations to put on it.'

'Can I ask Farida to come and join?' I know she'd definitely like to do this.

'Sure.'

'Now, Mak?'

'Yes. But see what they're doing in their house. If Farida is busy helping her mother, you'd better wait for another time.'

'OK, Mak.'

I run straight to Farida's house. She is giving her mother (who's lying on the carpet) a foot massage.

'A ha, it's Willa,' Farida's mother lifts her head from the pillow.

'Yes, Bude!' (Bude means Auntie. Mak says this is what I should call Farida's mum.)

'You're going to ask Farida if she wants to come and play, aren't you?'

'I want to make a Christmas tree, Bude.'

'A Christmas tree? Wow! I wonder how you make one of those. When?'

Farida has stopped massaging her mum's feet by now.

'Now.'

'Can I go, Mak?' Farida asks her mum (now sitting up).

'Ah, Christmas is already here. Yes, you can go, Farida,' says Farida's mum as she rolls onto her back. Farida gets up and stands next to me.

'Come on!' She takes my hand, so excited. Still holding hands, we race to my house.

When we get there, Farida whispers: 'How do you make a Christmas tree?'

'I've no idea. But Mak will teach us.'

In the living room, Mak is standing by the kitchen table, which is now laden with shiny paper, calendars, scissors, string, glue, crayons and little bottles of coloured powder. There are reels of cotton too, plus a finger bowl and a handkerchief.

'Ready?'

'Ready, Mak!'

The coloured powders are called kesumba and are what you mix with water to put the colour in cakes. I make clouds, stars, balloons and little boxes. Farida makes leaves and flowers. Mak makes chickens and cats.

And then we put everything on the tree's branches. Farida, Mak and I work and work until the day darkens. It's almost time for Maghrib,* so Mak tells us to stop working and go wash our hands. Pak will be home soon and Farida has to go and pray with her brothers and sisters.

* Maghrib – Muslim prayers at sunset

43

Chickenpox

Yesterday, after school, I went over to Farida's house.

I called her name over and over again but there was no answer.

When I opened the gate, her mother came outside to speak to me.

'Willa, I can't let Farida out at the moment. She has chickenpox.'

Chickenpox? What sort of illness is this?

'Sure, Bude,' I said. 'But can she still play with dolls?'

'Yes, she might be able to, but she has to play alone. If you play with her, you'll get infected. Now please go home. When she gets better, you two can play together again,' her mother explained, before saying goodbye.

So I went home alone. And Farida was alone too, playing on her own at her house.

I really wanted to show her the twinkling lights on our Christmas tree. Pak brought them from the office that afternoon.

The lights have a long cable that runs all the way round the branches and that you switch on at the base of the tree. And then, hey presto: you have an amazing Christmas tree. Farida would love it. But sadly she has chickenpox so can't go anywhere. I sat down on my own in front of the Christmas tree and watched the lights sparkle.

'Ah, you're home already? Did you go and play with Farida?'

'Nope. Her mum wouldn't let her outside.'

'Oh? Why's that?'

DIA SAKIT CACAR.

* She has chickenpox.

'Bude said she has chickenpox, so she has to stay at home.'

'Ah, that's right. If she has chickenpox, it's better that she stays at home. She can't play with anybody else.'

'Why, Mak?'

'Because you could get infected.'

'But what about Bude?'

'Well, chickenpox is the kind of illness that you can only get once in your life. If someone's already had it once, then they won't get it again. It's the same for me – I had chickenpox when I was small, so now I can go near

45

someone with it and not get infected.'

'What about me, Mak?'

'You've not had it, Willa.'

'I'd like to have it now, Mak.'

'Oh you really don't! Just like lots of other diseases, it makes you feel terrible. You get a fever. And you get these spots everywhere – all over your body. Sometimes you even get them on your head. There's a sort of nasty juice inside the spots which is really itchy. And if you scratch these spots then they pop and turn into scars. It's a really horrible illness, Willa.'

'But if I had chickenpox then at least I could still play with Farida, Mak…'

'If you *both* had chickenpox, you still couldn't play together. Because you'd be all itchy and you'd have a fever.'

'Ouch.'

'Yes, you just have to be patient. Now, I can read you some books if you like? Or you could play with Very Tiny Yellow Chick – where has he got to?'

Very Tiny Yellow Chick is outside. He seems busy, picking at the earth.

If I want to play with him, I have to catch him first. But now he can run faster and faster. I can never get close enough to catch him.

Mak hasn't bought any new books for me. So it would be the perfect time to play dolls with Farida. And under the twinkling tree.

Ugh. Why must chickenpox exist?

I really really *really* don't like it.

At Pak's office

When he gets back from church, Pak for once doesn't change out of his suit and dry out his mattress like he usually does on Sundays. Pak has to go to the office. Because not so long from now, it'll be the Christmas and New Year holidays and he has Important Work to do.

'How about taking Willa into the office?' Mak asks him.

'Would you like to go with Pak, Willa?' Mak asks me.

'Go to your office, Pak? Yes! I'd love to!'

I wonder what it looks like.

'Hmm, why don't you stay at home? There's nobody in the office, just Sie and me,' says Pak.

So Pak wants me to stay at home? No way. Now I really want to visit Pak's office. I can be his and Oom Sie's friend there. Absolutely.

'It's no big thing. Bring her along. So she can see your office. And maybe she'll learn something new,' Mak suggests.

Yep, I really want to explore Pak's office. What even is an office? Who is in there? Pak's friends? Are there any storybooks? Or toys?

'Learn what?' asks Pak.

Hmm, maybe I could learn to work like Pak. Or I could arrange the tables and chairs? Or organise the cupboards?

'Anything. She'll find something to do,' says Mak, playing with my hair.

'Hmmm… why can't she just stay with Mbok today?' asks Pak again. His voice has gone all high-pitched. He doesn't sound very happy.

'Nope. Not possible. She's visiting her niece who just had a baby. And I already have an appointment with Farida's mum to help her with some cooking. So Willa would be alone at home.'

'Farida?' asks Pak. His forehead looks all tight and knotted up.

'Chickenpox,' says Mak quickly.

I wonder why being ill with chickenpox takes a thousand years. I really want to play with Farida again. She needs to see the amazing lights on the tree. But I want to go with Pak to his office too. I get bored so fast at home. Mak still hasn't bought any new books. Maybe the library is shut or on holiday or the bookshop owner has caught chickenpox too. Maybe *that's* why we can't have anything new.

'Fine. Fine! Willa will come with me to the office,' says Pak.

I jump up around happily. But Pak is silent. His forehead still doesn't look quite normal just yet. He scratches his head. His hair, which always looks like toothbrush bristles, looks even stiffer than usual.

'Don't worry. I'll get everything she needs all ready, so you won't have to do much to take care of her,' says Mak, racing off to the kitchen.

Pak is looking at me and his eyebrows are very high. Weirdly high. And his eyes are looking very large.

'Shall I put my shoes on, Pak?'

He nods his head. 'Yes, but please wash your feet first. They look filthy,' and he points at my feet.

I go straight to the bathroom and wash my feet and put my sandals back on. Then I get my shoes from the place Mak has put them and race back to Pak.

Mak is waiting for us with a cloth bag in her hands.

'Her water bottle and her lunchbox are inside. She has spare clothes too, in case she gets her clothes wet.'

'Wet?'

'Yes, if she runs around and gets all sweaty, then you have to change her clothes or she might catch cold.'

Pak is nodding his head. He takes the bag from Mak and puts it over his shoulder.

Did Mak say that I could run around? Does Pak's office have a garden? Or a big yard? A yard even bigger than at school?

'Oh, there's a book here too?' Pak is rummaging around in the bag.

'Yes, so she can read if she gets tired running around,' says Mak, now combing my hair.

So there's a book inside the bag too? By now, I'm thinking that this yard is going to be so big we can play football there. And I'm going to see it.

Now Mak is walking with us out of the house.

Pak takes my hand and we walk to the corner of the alley.

'We'd better take a becak,' he says. There are two becaks waiting at the end of the alley. Pak chooses the one without the tarpaulin on top but, because it doesn't have a cover, whenever the wind blows my hair flies everywhere. I keep my eyes closed because of the wind and because of my hair blowing about. When the becak drives off I hear a weird buzzing sound. I know what it is though, as Mak once explained to me. It's the rubber underneath the becak, and when the becak driver is cycling and the wind is blowing, then this rubber buzzes.

Pak tells me that Johar Street isn't very far from our house. But it feels like it's miles away.

After turning left then right, then right then left, and the right and right and right and right and then… left… finally the becak arrives in front of a house with an enormous yard. Mak is right! I can run all over the place here!

'Come and get down, Willa,' says Pak, while he pays the driver.

I've never seen a house as big as this. There are all these giant windows. Pak pushes the gate open. It's different from the gate to my house – the fence here is ten times bigger and it's not made of wood. Pak is holding my hand.

A large door in the middle of the building is open.

Oom Sie appears from inside. He's wearing a short-sleeved white shirt and white trousers.

'Oh, so we have a special guest coming today. Will she be working with us?' he says, shaking my hand.

'Yes, her mother has an appointment with a neighbour. Her best friend has chickenpox and Mbok is visiting her niece. We won't be staying long, so I hope it's OK for me to bring her here with me.'

Oom Sie nods his head. He looks happy.

'But of course Willa can come and visit our office,' he says. 'How are you doing, Willa?' Oom Sie shakes my hand with a wide smile. He has big, even teeth. All of them are just a touch yellow.

'I'm alright, Oom.' I shake his hand too. His fingers are so long and thin. His palms feel cold. After we shake hands, he straightaway starts fiddling with his hair, which has already drooped over his face.

Pak and Oom Sie walk together into the house through the enormous door. I follow them. They talk to each other in a language I don't understand. I think it must be Dutch.

Passing through that big door, there's a large room with lots of chairs and tables. On each of the tables there are pieces of paper and these things… made of metal. Some of them are black and others are dark green. Each machine has bit of metal sticking out the side of it, the same size and shape as a spoon handle.

When I get closer to one of the tables, I spy that each of these machines also has a set of buttons with the letters of the alphabet on them. What on earth for? I try pulling at one of the buttons. It's too stiff. So I try pushing it instead and the button sinks down and I hear it go *tick*. At the same time as the button goes down, a metal stick inside stands up on end. I push another button and another one of the metal sticks stands up. I put my fingers together and cover as many of the alphabet buttons as I can. Suddenly… wow… lots and lots of the little metal sticks are all standing up on end. WOWEE.

'It's a typewriter, Willa. It's used for writing.' Pak is standing beside me. He lifts my hands from the machine and then carefully presses down all those little metal sticks which were standing up on end. So this machine is used to write things. Using those buttons and those sticks. But how does it work?

'Pak, I want to write something with this machine,' I say.

Then I hear Oom Sie's voice.

'Take her to your desk, Koh Thio!'

'Do you want to see my desk now, or after you've had a chance to run around, Willa?'

A chance to run around… The thing is, I can run around any time, any place. But I can only play with these tick-tick-tick machines in Pak's office. So I think I'd better play with one of the machines. Right here, right now.

Pak walks away from the table and past all these other tables and typewriters. I follow him until we arrive at the front of the room. Pak reaches into his pocket, brings out a key, and opens the door to the room.

'So this is my office. And this is my desk…' he says.

Inside the room is a not-so-big table, and on the table there proudly sits a big black typewriter. The metal stalks that stick out of it are bigger than the other typewriters. And the alphabet buttons are white, with a tinge of yellowy-brown all round the edges.

'Is this your typewriter, Pak?'

'It's the office's, but I use it every day to do my work,' says Pak as he opens the glass door to a bookcase, looking for something there. He shuts the bookcase then goes to the table and looks there. He can't seem to find the thing he needs. He's squatting down now, opening up the drawers of the desk.

'A ha, there you are!' Pak shouts. He is beaming. He leans back at his desk, jubilant, and starts to read the papers. Then he takes out a cigarette and starts smoking.

Oh DRAT. I knew it. Once he's started smoking, this means he'll be reading for ages.

'Pak…' I sit down in his chair, in front of the machine. 'Hmmmm….'

Pak is still smoking and reading. I wonder if I can write something on this special machine without any instructions.

'Come *on*, Pak… Let's write something!'

I pat the top of Pak's desk.

'What was that? Oh, writing something with the typewriter? OK! Let's do it.'

Pak takes a sheet of paper and tucks it round the little sideways tube at the top of the machine.

Crack-crack-crack, Pak turns the tube at the side.

The paper pops out of the top.

He pulls the handle, the paper pops up, and Pak starts pushing the buttons. Fast. And I mean *fast*. The little metal sticks are jumping up and down like mad.

'Willa, look!' Pak points at the paper in the machine. It now has something written on it. It looks just like the writing in a book or a newspaper.

'Today Willa came to the office with Pak… and I really wanted to use this tick-tick-ticking machine…' I read the writing typed on the piece of paper. Pak is giggling.

He pulls the metal handle and the paper pops up again.

Pak starts pushing the alphabet buttons again and making more writing.

I start laughing when I read what it says: 'Are you ready to write using this tick-tick-ticking machine?'

'I want to try it now, Pak!'

Pak nods his head and pulls the metal handle again.

I put all ten of my fingers on the buttons. I push them as hard as I can so that lots of the metal sticks start jumping about.

'It doesn't really work like that, Willa. You have to look at the letters on the buttons and then push them one by one,' explains Pak.

'But I want to use it like you do…'

'A ha… If you want type quickly like this…' Pak talks to me at the same time as he types, without even looking at the keys, '… then you have to practise and learn for a long time. A very very long time. But since you've only just met this machine, it's better to push the buttons one by one. Here, I'll show you how you do it one by one. The trick is to do it slowly.'

This I can do.

So I choose the letters I want to use and I push them one by one. Hooray! I did it. But why are all my words lumped together into one long sentence, not like Pak's writing or the writing you see in books?

'Ah, I forgot to tell you… every time you finish a word, you have to push the space bar… the long one. Come on, try it.'

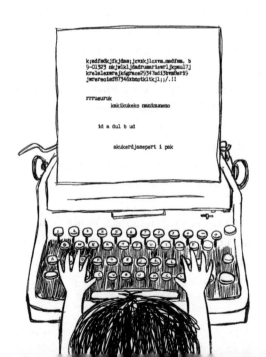

Pak is right. Every time I push the space bar, the words are no longer joined up.

this – space – is – space – pak – space – office – space
pak – space – mak – space – farida – space – dul

Victory.

All that afternoon I am so busy typing that I forget to run about in the yard. After a while I stop and eat the lunch Mak made me. And that is only because Pak reminded me – otherwise I'd have just carried on typing.

Pak has finished his work for the day now. He tells me it's time to go home.

Now? But I want to stay at Pak's office.

I haven't finished my typing.

'How about we go home a bit later, Pak?'

'Hmm, I think it's better we go home now. It's getting dark. Come and get ready.'

So I have to leave the typewriter?

'Er, Pak… Can we take the typewriter home?'

'No we can't, Willa. The office owns the typewriter. Come on, it's time.'

So I really do have to go home. And I can't bring the typewriter home. I decide I'll have to come back to Pak's office very soon.

'What about the paper, Pak? Could I bring that home?' I ask.

'Of course. Let me help you get it ready. We can show Mak what you got up to at my office.'

We take the pieces of paper I've been typing, fold them up and slide them into an envelope.

'Can I come back to your office again another day?'

'Certainly.'

'And can I use this machine again, Pak?'

'Sure!'

I am happy as can be.

Pak and Oom Sie leave the office together.

Pak and I are going back home by becak.

Oom Sie is riding on his bicycle. The one that goes tick-tick-tick every time he pushes the pedals down.

I really want us to get home quickly.

I really want to tell Mak all about the typewriter.

And I also need to tell Mak that I can't go to school tomorrow because I'm going to come to Pak's office instead.

At home, Mak is busy cooking, warming up some food.

'Mak, I wrote with the typewriter at Pak's office. I typed so many things – so many words, Mak. Tick-tick-tick! And to stop the words all sticking together, there's something called the space bar. Tick! Which means the letters don't all get stuck together. And when you are about to reach the end of a line, the machine goes TIIIIIING. That means you have to pull the special handle, so the paper rolls down. Tick-tick-tick.'

'Wow, that sounds fun!'

'It was. Would you like to read the words I wrote, Mak?'

'Yes, I'd love to. Where are they?'

Pak is already standing next to me. He hands me all the bits of paper.

Mak reads them one by one.

She is laughing, overjoyed. 'This is brilliant!'

'Mak, I really love typing.'

'Well yes, this I can see.'

'I want to do more and more and more typing, Mak.'

'Of course.'

'Can I do it again tomorrow, Mak?'

'Tomorrow?'

'Yes, I was thinking I could go into the office with Pak tomorrow so I can do some more typing.'

'Hmm, tomorrow is a school day. And tomorrow's a work day too: Pak will be so busy. Maybe next week. Now, please take a shower then we'll eat afterwards. It's milkfish for dinner.'

Why would I want to have a shower? It's not as if I'm going anywhere.

And why would I want to eat? I'm not even hungry.

All I want to do is T Y P E.

Left Right

Farida is starting to get better. But I still can't play with her. Besides, I'm very busy. I'm even too busy to ride Poni.

I want to do some colouring in the book my teacher gave me – the one I'm allowed to bring home from school and draw in. I have to take it back tomorrow so Bu Guru can see what I've done. I was actually supposed to colour in this book at school, but I hadn't finished it when the bell rang. I really really love colouring. And I can usually do it turbo fast. But today… today is different.

When I get home from school, I go to the kitchen table, open my bag and take out a pencil and my drawing book.

'What are you doing, Willa?'

Ah, Mak is standing behind me. She holds my right hand and helps, because the colouring pencils keep slipping out of my hand.

'I keep losing my grip, Mak. It came out of my hand again. It won't let me hold onto it. See?'

'That's funny. Usually you're pretty good with a pencil?'

'Yes, but it feels… all sort of…weird.'

'Weird? Which one feels weird?'

'This one, Mak… This hand is all wobbly and strange when it holds the pencil. Look, Mak. Not this hand. *This hand* can hold the pencil really firmly. But the other one is all weird.'

I show Mak how my other hand feels all strange and wobbly when I hold the pencil.

'Well, sure. It feels strange because you're not used to holding a pencil with that hand. So that hand is still learning how to hold the pencil. But why are you using that one? Why aren't you using the hand you usually use?'

'Well *that* hand is the same hand all my friends use, Mak.'

'The same hand as your friends? What on earth does that mean?' Mak is holding up the red colouring pencil.

'My friends all do their colouring with *this* hand,' I try to explain to Mak, 'but I use the other hand.' I hold up the other one. 'And I wanted to be like my friends.' Oh… the pencil slides away again. It slips along the table then drops onto the floor. The tip is broken.

Mak picks two pencils up from the table.

One for me. One for Mak.

'Now, can you hold it with your other hand, Willa?'

I hold the pencil and it stays in my hand. It doesn't run away. Mak gives me a bit of paper from the calendar that she tears a page off every day.

'Now, let's write something. You write your name and I'll write my name.'

'But which hand should I use, Mak?'

'The hand you normally use every day. And I'll write with the hand I use every day too.'

I write my name. Mak writes her name.

I spy that Mak uses the same hand as me.

I am just like Mak! And Mak is just like me.

'Left hand. Right hand. It's all the same, Willa. Use the one you like – the one that you'd normally use to pick up a pencil.'

'I like this hand. The same as yours.'

'Yes, we both use the same hand.'

'But I don't use the same hand as all my friends, Mak.'

'But why should you be the same as your friends? This is *your* hand. This is *my* hand. We use the hand that feels most comfortable. The one that's strongest to hold a pencil and scissors. The hand that doesn't feel strange,' says Mak, looking at me with big wide eyes. 'Right hand. Left hand. There's no difference. They are both our hands. And it might be different from other people but it's alright. It's no big thing at all.'

So the two of us, me and Mak, we write and draw all sorts of things, until those pieces of paper are absolutely crammed full.

And I finish all my colouring homework for Ibu Juwita. I do it using a different hand from all my friends. But I use the same hand as Mak.

Reading

When I get home from school, Mak isn't there.

Mbok says she's gone to Nyonya Chang's office.

'Mak said you can go to Farida's house to play,' says Mbok.

Ah, Farida's not been here since yesterday. She went with her mother to visit Mbak Tini in Jember. Mbak Tini is often ill.

I go looking for Dul and Bud. Drat: Bud isn't allowed out because he has a fever. He's coughing and his nose is running. So I can only play with Dul. From a way off I can see him sitting on the balé-balé* at the front of his house. His walking stick is leant against the side of the seat.

'Where's Bud?' Dul calls out.

'He's sick.'

'Eugh. He's always sick. He constantly has a runny nose…'

'Where's your false leg, Dul?'

'Oh it's in the house. It's too heavy.'

One of Dul's legs is made of wood. It's a replacement, after his leg was cut off in a train accident a long time ago.

'What sort of game shall we play, Dul?'

'A game? I don't want to play any games. I'm not in the mood for marbles. I'm worn out from getting up and sitting again. Getting up and sitting down. Not to mention if my stick slips.'

---

* balé-balé – a type of outdoor seat, usually made from wood or bamboo and often with a small roof

'I can help you hold onto your stick!'

'Too complicated.'

'How about we play kites then?'

'It's not kite season, Willa. It's no fun if it's just us and there are no other kites.'

'So what shall we play instead?'

'We're not going to play anything. We'll just sit here like this, OK? This breeze feels so good,' says Dul, lazing on the balé-balé. His eyes are nearly closed.

Hmmm. What's so fun about sitting about?

'If this is what we're doing, then I'm going home.'

'Don't do that!'

'OK… So what are we going to play, then?'

When I start climbing down off the balé-balé, Dul gets up, grabs my hand and says, 'Don't go home now! OK, I know what will we do. Wait a minute!'

Dul clambers down from the balé-balé without his stick. He hops back to his house and returns with a cloth bag.

'Come and sit down.' He takes out some school textbooks and holds up one with a coconut tree on it. The cover says: *Ilmu Bumi Pulau Jawa. The Geography of the Island of Java.*

Dul flicks through the pages, stopping on one that looks like it has a big splodge of coffee spilt on it. At the top of the page it says: *Jakarta*.

'This is the one. Could you read it out, please? Loudly, OK?'

'Jakarta?' A ha, isn't that where my dad's always off to?

'Yep, it's about Jakarta. And I have a test on it tomorrow so please read it aloud. This is a science book for fourth graders. If you can read this, you're the smartest of all your friends. Come on, read! And don't forget to use a big loud voice,' he says, while lying down on the balé-balé. 'Come on, read it! What're you waiting for?'

'But what's this picture?'

On the page are all these lines and the words CENTRAL JAKARTA, WEST JAKARTA, EAST JAKARTA...

'It's a map of Jakarta. If you were looking at Jakarta from inside an aeroplane, this is what it'd look like.'

Right, so the coffee spill is Jakarta? It really doesn't look all that great. And who drew a load of spilt coffee and called it Jakarta?

'Eugh, stop asking all these questions! It'll make sense when you reach fourth grade. But for now, just read it. OK? I am all ears.'

So that's what fourth graders learn about: coffee spills.

'Come on, fusspot. READ IT.'

Very slowly, I read out the page in a loud voice:

> *The province of Jakarta. Bays and capes: Jakarta*
> *Bay, Krawang Cape. Port: Tanjung Priuk. Airport:*

Kemayoran. Islands: Onrust Island, Damar Island. Rivers: Cikande, Ciliwung, and Citarum. Places: Jakarta City, Jatinegara, Krawang, Tangerang, Bekasi.

Tangerang is famous for its weaving, including woven bamboo hats. In Tangerang, there is also a Young Offenders Unit. This is for youths who have committed crimes but are too young to go to prison as they cannot be punished like adults.

Dul listens with his eyes closed, his mouth murmuring the words as I read aloud – about Jakarta and the children's prison and the bamboo weaving.

A letter from my teacher

When we finish our lessons this afternoon, Ibu Guru gives each of us a little envelope. Bu Guru says we should give these envelopes to our parents when we get home. And they should be read as soon as possible then signed, and then we should bring them back to school.

'What's inside, Bu Guru?' I try to peek inside the white envelope that's all sealed up.

'Oh, it's an information letter for Mak about the radio schedule, Willa.'

'What's on the radio, Bu?'

'Ah, be patient… Let Mak tell you all about it once she's read it, OK?' Bu Guru tells me with the biggest of smiles.

I'm itching to know what's in this envelope but Ibu Guru says only Mak and Pak are allowed to open it and read what's inside. And after that, they have to decide if they agree or disagree with it. Agree with what? What is this all about? And why was my teacher talking about the radio schedule?

'Maaaaaaak! Maaaaaaaak!'

'What on earth's going on? Why have you been shrieking at me from all that way away?'

Mak opens the door looking surprised.

'This! THIS.' I give her the letter from Ibu Guru.

'What's this?'

AHHHG. Mak, it's a letter from Ibu Guru. Just hurry up and open it!

'Come on, Mak. Open the letter. Please read it now!

Ibu Guru said something about a radio program! Erres Radio, Mak? Is that right? Yes? Is it is it is it?

'OK OK, hold your horses.' Mak carefully opens the envelope. I wait. Pleeeease hurry up, Mak.

And then I see Mak smile a huge smile.

'Hurray!' she says in a very happy voice.

'Mak!'

'Willa, you're going to sing on the radio!' says Mak, picking me up and lifting me into the air. She hugs me tight. Oh, oh, oh, OH so that's what the letter from Bu Guru says: I'm going to sing on the radio!

Mak puts me down. We hold hands and jump up and down together.

'Now, Mak? Tomorrow?'

'Not now. Next week. Today is Tuesday and next Tuesday you'll be on the radio!'

'Am I actually going to be inside the radio?'

Mak says that inside the radio there's just electricity and wires and tiny little lights. Apparently no one actually gets inside it. Mak is really laughing now. She says: 'It's not you who gets on or in the radio, Willa… It's just your voice.'

'How does my voice end up in there, Mak?'

'Through radio frequencies, Willa. So when you sing at Radio Republic Indonesia, I hope that Mak, Mbok, Dul, Farida, Bud, and also Pak will be able to hear your voice in their homes and in the office.'

This is seriously big news.

Ida, Dul, Bud, Mak, Mbok, Pak… All these people will hear my voice on the radio, just like when I hear Lilis

MASUK RADIO?

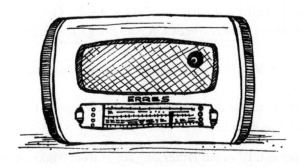

* Get inside the radio?

Suryani's voice. I'm so happy I race out of the house to find Dul, Ida and Bud.

But I can't find them.
    They're not back from school yet.
    Ahh.

Walking back home, I start thinking: where will I be when I sing on the radio? What sort of song will I sing? I wonder if I can sing 'Three Nights'. Oh no, that one's too long. And it's an extremely sad song. So what sort of song should I sing?

At home, I ask Mak what kind of song I should sing next week.

'All the songs that Bu Guru has taught you. You can sing those, Willa.'

'How about I sing 'Teluk Bayur',* Mak?'

'Hmmm, 'Teluk Bayur' doesn't quite… fit… into a children's radio programme,' says Mak.

'But I…'

'Yes?'

'But I'm really not a big fan of the songs Bu Guru has taught us. *My hat is round. Round is my hat. If it's not round…*'

'*It's not Willa's hat,*' Mak finishes the song, laughing. Loudly.

Round hat. Hat that's round. My hat. Not my hat. I'm round. I'm not round…

To be honest, I'd much rather sing songs from Mak's record collection. When will I get to sing those songs? I am getting properly fed up with all this *my hat is round. The cat with three stripes. Waking up and brushing my teeth…*

---

* Teluk Bayur – Teluk Bayur is the name of a port in West Sumatra, and also the title of a popular love song.

On the radio

A week can seem a really long time.

Before we reach Tuesday, there's first got to be Wednesday-Thursday-Friday-Saturday-Sunday-Monday. It's a long long time.

Our teacher has taught us the first song we're going to sing on the radio.

> *Good afternoon Bu, good afternoon Pak,*
> *good afternoon all my friends.*
> *We're happy to meet you here, all together,*
> *on Radio Surabaya.*

Ever since learning this song, I've sung it almost every day. Mbok, Mak and possibly even Very Tiny Yellow Chick all know it off by heart. Dul now covers his ears when he hears it. He says it's *boring*.

A ha, and I've learnt another song, that I'm going to sing by myself and not with any of my classmates.

> *In a flower garden,*
> *such a beautiful place,*
> *we play together*
> *and have fun.*
> *Everywhere*
> *jasmines and roses,*
> *here and there,*
> *the sweetest perfume.*

SELAMAT SORE BU
SELAMAT SORE PAK...

CIAP CIAP CIAP

* Good afternoon Bu
  Good afternoon Pak...

At long last, we reach TUESDAY, the big day when I'm going to be singing on the national radio station, RRI Surabaya.

In the morning, just like any other day, we learn the usual sort of stuff at school. And we go home at the usual time too. The important message from Ibu Juwita is that everyone has to be at the studio at 4 o'clock in the afternoon. But before 4 o'clock, Mak says I have to have a little rest (meaning I have to take proper nap) so that later on I sing perfectly. But my eyes just don't want to go to sleep. And I'm afraid that if I do fall asleep then I'll miss when I'm supposed to go to the radio station.

'OK, OK, if you can't fall asleep, try just lying down instead. Don't go running around.'

'Can I read, Mak?'

'Sure, but if you must read something, do it sitting down, Willa.'

But I can't read anything. I feel like I've read all the books. I don't know what to do with myself. Ah, no… I do know what I want to do with myself. I want to go straight to the radio station and start singing.

We go by becak and reach the station at half-past three.

Joko, Gatot and Asih are already there. Eko, Sri and Ita all arrive after me. Endang gets there last of all. Her face is all white and her lips are all red. So Endang is wearing lipstick now!

Me? I don't have any lipstick on. I don't even have any of that scented powder on. But before I have a chance to tell Mak about Endang's red lips, Ibu Guru claps her hands and tells us to go on into the building.

This place is LARGE. The ceilings are so high that they're far away. It's cold here. We're led into the room with grey walls that are full of holes. Inside the room are three metal poles with a round thing at the end of each of them. Two of the poles aren't particularly high – just a little bit taller than me. But the other one, the one which has an even bigger round thing on it, is really really tall.

In one corner, there's a small glass room. A lady is sitting in there with lots of books set in front of her. Her ears are covered by two rubber bowls. Why has she put a pair of bowls on her ears? And if her ears are covered by rubber bowls, how does she expect to hear me and my friends?

Ibu Guru gathers us in another corner of the room and explains that the lady in the glass room is going to read out some stories. Before she tells the first story, we are going to sing our 'Good afternoon' song and then she will tell another story before we sing our next song.

Ibu Guru calls us to attention and organises us so we know when to sing. She's going to give us a SIGN when we have to start. But I suddenly realise that Mak and all the other mothers aren't here. They didn't come with us! Where are they? Ibu Guru comes up to me and puts a hand on my shoulder. 'Willa, so you're going to sing the flower garden song later, yes? Now, do you know all the words off by heart?'

Heck. My feet have gone cold. I feel like there's a sweet stuck in my throat. I keep swallowing my saliva over and over again. What if the words to the song fly out of my head? What if…

'Of course you can,' says my teacher with a big smile, all the while patting my shoulder. 'It's a nice and easy song, right?' she says.

Yes but… why does my throat feel so dry? And why are my hands are all clammy and sweaty? What if I forget the song? What if I get halfway through it and then forget everything? What if…

And then my turn arrives. Ibu Juwita holds my hand. 'Stay calm! Of course you can do it. You've practised this song every day. Don't worry,' she whispers, winking at me.

What I really want is Mak beside me. I turn to look at the entrance to the room. But Mak isn't there. My teacher is crouched in front of me. Her hands are holding my shoulders. She looks straight into my eyes. 'You're looking for Mak? She's just outside. And do you know what, she's waiting to hear you sing on the radio. So you'd better sing loud and clear for Mak. OK, Willa?'

I nod my head. Yes, I do want to sing for Mak. And also for Pak, who Mak said would be listening in at the office with Oom Sie's radio.

And then a man comes up to me carrying a metal chair with a rattan back, that he puts in front of the tallest metal pole. 'Come up onto this,' he says, offering me his hand.

'The microphone stand can't go any lower, so you have to stand on a chair so you can sing into the mic with your lovely sweet voice,' says Ibu Guru.

I climb up. And they're right, the big funnel thing that's called a microphone now sits just in front of my mouth. But before I finish inspecting it, my teacher gives me the SIGN to start singing the song I've been practising all week.

In a flower garden…

I don't even realise that I've finished singing. My friends, my teacher, the man who brought me the chair and the lady with the rubber bowls are all clapping and clapping their hands. WOW.

I climb down off the chair and join my friends. We sing the first song again altogether and then it's all finished.

My clothes are all wet on my back. And my socks inside my shoes. Sweat!

The big door opens and Mak is standing up there with the biggest smile I've ever seen in my whole life. I run and

73

jump into her arms. 'I heard your voice on the radio, Willa!' she whispers to me. I am so happy. Yep, right now I am the happiest person in the universe.

From that day on, my friends and I carry on singing at RRI Surabaya. I often sing on my own too, standing on that chair in front of the microphone with the round thing on it. Oh, and the lady with the rubber bowls? Yep, she's always there too.

It turns out those rubber bowls actually mean she can hear everything extra clear. My teacher told me all about them.

Mak sometimes listens at home. And sometimes she likes to hear my voice in the RRI waiting room. Pak and Oom Sie always listen in with the radio at the office. And then Dul, Bud, Farida and her mum all listen in on their radios at home.

Bu Juwita teaches us new songs each week that we're going to sing on RRI. So now I know absolutely masses of songs. But really I want to sing things like 'Hesti' or 'Teluk Bayur'. Or… really anything at all so long as it isn't 'The Round Hat' or 'The Cat with Three Stripes'. Unfortunately, I'm just not allowed. Bu Guru says that 'Hesti', 'Tiga Malam' and 'Sangkuriang' are not the sort of songs that children are supposed to sing.

And then Endang… Well, whenever she sings on the radio, she still puts on all this white face powder and lipstick. But Mak *still* says that make-up – and lipstick especially – isn't for children.

* In the flower garden...

Tante Lan #1

This morning, before school, Mak tells me that Tante Lan is going to visit our house.

'When, Mak?'

'Maybe two or three days from now. Let's ask Pak later.'

Tante Lan is Pak's younger sister who used to live in Jakarta. Her real name is Mey Lan but Pak has always called her Lan. She's the person who sent me my gorilla doll. It's been a long long time since Pak has seen her. Mak tells me that Tante Lan has left Jakarta and now lives in Singapore.

'Is Singapore far away, Mak?'

'Yes, it's pretty far. We'd have to go by plane from here. Or we could take a big ship, like that one we saw in Tanjung Perak. But it'd take a couple of weeks to get to Singapore. If we took a plane we'd be there in just a few hours.'

Mak says, Tante Lan is working in Singapore while she carries on studying. She lives by herself there.

'Doesn't she have any friends?'

'Oh, she has lots of friends!'

'But she's on her own, Mak.'

'Well, 'on her own' just means that she lives by herself in her house. But even there she's not totally on her own, because she lives with her dog…who's called… Hmm, now what's his name again…'

'Her dog that goes woof-woof-woof, Mak?'

'Yes, that's the one.'

'Is Tante Lan's dog really big, Mak?'

'Hold on a tick, let's have a look at the picture she sent us.'

Mak opens up the drawer under the radio. She takes out a blue envelope with all these red and blue patterns on it and the words PAR AVION. Mak's name is on the front of the envelope. 'Tan Mey Lan' is written on the back of it. Then there are some numbers and some writing that says 'Tiong Bahru'. Mak takes out a folded sheet of blue paper and there inside is a photo of a young woman with long hair down to her shoulders, standing in front of some brightly-coloured flowers. In her hand is a lead, tethered to the neck of a brown dog who's sitting up straight. His tongue is wagging and he looks very jolly.

'So this is Tante Lan. And this is...' Mak turns the photo over. 'Puff!' Mak passes me the photo. I look at it closely then flip it over to read what's written on the back.

'What does the word 'me' mean, Mak?'

'It means 'aku'. And this word 'and' means 'dan', and well, 'Puff' means 'Puff'.'

'How come it says 'me' though, Mak?'

'It's because Tante Lan wrote it in English.'

'English?'

A ha, this is the language that's in all those books Pak brought back from Jakarta.

'In English, they say 'I' and 'you' and 'cat' and 'dog'.'

'What about ayam, Mak?'

'Ayam is chicken.'

Hmmm, English is weird.

Ayam is chicken.

Kucing is cat.

'What about bebek?'

'Duck.'

'Dak, Mak?'

'Well yes, Willa: duck.'

I really don't get English.

Why does a bebek have to be called a duck? Why is a kucing a cat and an ayam a chicken?

Mak is gathering up Tante Lan's letter with all those words I don't understand and slipping it back inside the envelope.

Suddenly my heart starts beating really fast and really hard.

'Mak... Does Tante Lan speak English the whole time?'

'Yes. Yes, she speaks English and Chinese.'

Oh! Oh NO.

'But I can't speak English, Mak.'

'I'm not so great at English either, Willa. Pak is excellent at speaking other languages, though.'

'Can't she speak Javanese, Mak?'

'Hmmmm, as I recall she can't really speak Javanese. But I think she can speak Indonesian because she lived in Jakarta for all that time. We can ask Pak.'

Ask Pak? WHEN? Do we have to wait until he gets home? That is ages away. I really want to ask him now.

> Kucing... Cat...
> Ayam... Chicken...
> Rumah... House...
> Bebek... Duck...
> Anjing... Dog...

But what if I want to tell Tante Lan stories about school? Or about Farida? Or Dul? Or flying my kite? How am I going to tell her? Sigh.

Why o why o why o why isn't Pak home yet?

Tante Lan #2

Pak is so busy at the moment.

When I leave for school, he hasn't woken up.

Mak says he got home so late last night that we'd best let him sleep.

The night after, I wait up for Pak.

But he doesn't come home until I've already gone to bed.

I don't have a chance to ask him about English for two whole days.

When I get home from school in the afternoon, I have a thumping headache.

'Maybe I'm just hungry, Mak.'

'Hmmm, this is one possibility. But *another possibility* is that you're thinking so much about learning English,' says Mak.

Ah now, this is indeed possible. Yep. I have a headache and feel all dizzy because I'm not going to be able to tell Tante Lan any stories when she come to our house this evening.

After we eat nasi urap,* Mak says that I should nap for a while. Mak promises to wake me up when Tante Lan arrives.

'But I'm not sleepy, Mak.'

I'm never sleepy in the afternoon.

'Well, you need to have a rest in your room to stop that headache.'

---

* nasi urap – rice with vegetables

I go to my room and climb onto the bed. I open my eyes as wide as they'll stretch, because I only want to rest and not actually go to sleep. But (of course) I nod off. When I wake up, I can hear Pak's voice outside my bedroom door. A ha, does this mean Tante Lan has already arrived? Oh no oh no oh no. How did this happen?

I race out of my room, but in the living room there's only Mak and Pak. Where's Tante Lan? Did she change her plans?

'No no no, you're awake already! Now, you have a shower, Willa! We're going to pick up Tante Lan,' says Pak.

Pick up Tante Lan?

Now?

I sprint off to the bathroom and Mak runs after me, laying out my clothes.

Ahhg. The water is absolutely freezing. But that's OK as I am going to have the world's fastest shower so I can be ready to go. Mak explains that Pak has borrowed a car so we can collect Tante Lan from the airport. Mak laughs as she watches me scurry about.

We walk down the alley to where the car is parked. Mak sits up front with Pak and I sit in the backseat with Gorilla (the toy that Tante Lan sent me). The car zooms and zooms. The wind whooshes into the car and blows my hair all over the place. I feel like it takes us absolutely ages to get to the airport.

When we arrive, we park the car and Pak leads us over to a fence where we can watch the planes landing. There's one plane that's moving slowly.

'Look! The plane just landed,' says Pak, pointing at this aeroplane that's slowing down and has now stopped completely.

Suddenly a door on the side of the plane opens up, and one by one people emerge. Pak is pointing to a tall woman in black trousers and a white shirt, with a scarf on her head tied under her chin. She's wearing black sunglasses and holding a brown suitcase.

'There she is! Tante Lan! Tante Lan!' says Pak.

Mak and I start waving frantically. Pak does all this loud whistling. And Tante Lan turns her head. She waves at us and even from where I'm standing all that way away, I can see that she's smiling a huge smile.

Pak then guides me and Mak forwards, and in no time at all Tante Lan is here with us. Pak and Tante Lan hug one another, and then Mak joins the hug, and then… Tante Lan crouches down in front of me and, as she takes off her big black sunglasses, she says (in Indonesian), 'Good afternoon, Willa. How are you?'

Oh! I can barely breathe. Tante Lan is asking me how I am.

Mak touches my hand. 'Willa, Tante Lan has asked you how you're feeling.'

I answer quickly. 'I feel great, Tante.'

'That's wonderful. Really, truly wonderful,' she replies.

And then she takes my hand. Pak has his arm round Mak's waist and they set off back to the car. Tante Lan and I hold hands, following them.

Once we're in the car, I sit in the back with Tante Lan. In the front seat, Pak whistles and Mak hums along.

Tante Lan takes off her sunglasses and I see that her eyes are just like Pak's eyes. Narrow. She takes her scarf off too and her hair tumbles down onto her shoulders. It's black, thick and falls straight, like the rain.

'Now, I hear that Willa is already at school. Is that so?' she asks me.

'Yes, I am. I go to Kindergarten Juwita,' I reply.

'That's wonderful. Really, truly wonderful.' she says, smiling away.

I tell her all about Ida and about the Gorilla she sent me and about the books in my teacher's bookcase and the black horse that Pak gave me. Tante Lan's eyes open very wide when I tell her about singing on the radio.

'That's absolutely brilliant,' she says, clapping her hands and hugging me. I'm feeling pretty great. Tante Lan then tells me all about Puff, the dog with the brown fur who was on the photo she sent Mak.

I can't understand everything she says, because there are so many words I'm hearing for the very first time. But there are some I know already: Yes and No and Excellent…

That night, I tell Mak that perhaps it'd be best if I stay home from school so I can carry on talking to Tante Lan. I want to hear more of her stories. And, of course, I want to learn English from her. But Mak says I still have to go to school. I keep my fingers crossed that when I get back Tante Lan is still here and we can carry on chatting about absolutely everything.

As soon as school is over, I run as fast as my legs will go so I get home quickly. Luckily, Tante Lan is still here. She's in the kitchen with Mak and Mbok. Mbok is cooking rawon[*] today. Mbok is like me: she can't really speak English.

---

[*] rawon – a dark soup made of beef and seasoned with keluak, a black nut that gives the soup its unusual colour

That's why Mak is explaining the recipe to Tante Lan: about how to mix up the ingredients and how you use keluak nuts to make rawon. Tante Lan carefully notes down the recipe. I sit down next to her. She writes and writes, then smiles across at me – and just like that (and just like Pak), her eyes vanish.

Late in the afternoon, Pak gets home. Outside the house, I can hear Farida calling me. Yes, it's been a couple of days since I've played with her or Bud.

The thing is, I'm just so busy with Tante Lan. It's not every day that she's here, right? And what if all of a sudden she has to go home?

In the dining room, Mak has laid out all the plates. The rawon is all ready to eat and Mbok tells us that the meat is perfectly tender. We sit round the table ready to eat.

I love rawon. It smells dee-licious. Mbok says that if you want to make good rawon, then you have to cook the meat for a whole day so it becomes all tender, and so the spices taste just right. Rawon is perfect to eat with warm rice, a spicy sort of sauce called sambal terasi, prawn crackers and bean sprouts, all topped with an egg. Mbok makes me some sambal too. In a little bowl, she mixes up red chilli (without its seeds), shrimp, salt and lots of tomatoes. It is HOT. But eaten alongside rawon it's absolutely delicious. I have two helpings.

After dinner, Tante Lan stands up and says she wants to hear me sing.

Mak stands next to Tante Lan, smiling a great big smile.

What sort of song should I sing?

'You can sing whatever you want,' says Pak.

'Can I sing 'Hesti'?'

'Of course you can,' says Mak.

Ah, not 'Hesti'…

Yes, I know what sort of song I'd like Tante Lan to hear.
But before I sing it, there's something I have to get ready.
I race to the kitchen to look for a barrel (where Mak keeps
the rice). When I come back from the kitchen, Mak has
already got me a chair to stand on. I sing something I heard
on the radio a long time ago with Mak:

This is the story of the magnificent Sangkuriang
who one day met the most beautiful princess.
Sangkuriang was flushed with romance,
Sangkuriang proposed to the princess.

The princess was shocked by a scar on Sangkuriang's head,
for it so happened that Sangkuriang was none other but her son.
Oh… the princess begged God
to block everything.
Sangkuriang's heart was broken.

And this is the story
of the people of Priangan.

I sing this all while standing on a chair. In my hand, a
bit like a microphone, is the funnel Mak and Mbok use
to measure rice, which I took from the barrel. When I've
finished singing, Tante Lan, Pak, Mak and Mbok all burst
into applause. And then we sing along together:

The twinkling lights of the ship
A shipmate plays on the lifeboat
Tears fall on the pillow, oh!

Tante Lan claps her hands then hugs me and Mak together. I'm so so happy.

After singing together, Pak invites Tante Lan to come outside. She's a smoker too, just like Pak. Mak goes and joins them on the terrace, talking and writing a little. They all talk in English.

I take my small chair and sit beside Mak.

I don't know what on earth they're talking about. They are laughing and laughing together.

What's so funny?

Hmm, maybe I should just go to Farida's house. She won't have started praying just yet.

But in the end I just stay sitting quietly next to Mak.

I love hearing Tante Lan's voice when she laughs.

Cing coang

The next evening, Pak takes me, Tante Lan and Mak to Jembatan Merah.* We go there in two becaks. One for Pak and me. One for Mak and Tante Lan. When we arrive, we stop at a little food stall on wheels, lit by a paraffin lamp. In the window of the stall it says Bakmi Pangsit Jembatan Merah, which means 'Red Bridge Noodle Dumplings'. Pak takes four wooden chairs for us then goes to speak to the stallholders: two young women with pale skin and narrow eyes that look just like Pak and Tante Lan's eyes. Pak holds up four fingers but I don't know what he's ordered because Pak is speaking in a language I've never heard before. To me it sounds something like cing-coang-cing-coang.

'Mak...' I whisper in Mak's ear. 'What language is Pak speaking in?'

'Pak has ordered us four big bowls of pangsit noodles. He's speaking in Chinese to the ladies who sell the noodles.'

'Can you speak Chinese?'

'I can't speak any Chinese. One day we should learn to speak it, Willa.'

'Will Pak teach us?'

'Yes, who else?' says Mak, winking at me.

'Cing coang, Mak?'

'Yes, if Pak isn't too busy, we'll learn cing coang,' says Mak, giggling to herself.

---

* Jembatan Merah – 'Red Bridge' – a famous bridge in Surabaya that connects the two halves of the city, that was also the site of fierce fighting during Indonesia's battle for independence

Teddy Bea

This morning, the day after we had those noodles at Jembatan Merah, Pak and Tante Lan head off somewhere in the car very early. There's no time for me to see them at all.

Mak says that Tante Lan asked Pak to take her to Malang to catch up with an old friend. She also has some business to attend to there.

'When she's visited Malang, will Tante Lan come back to our house, Mak?'

'I'm afraid she won't have time for that, Willa. Tante Lan will have to go straight to the airport.'

'When will she be back, Mak?'

'I don't know, Willa. Tante Lan is so busy with work.'

'But will she come back at some point, Mak?'

'Yes, maybe someday.'

'But when *is* that someday, Mak? Is it tomorrow or a long time from now?'

'Hmm, I suppose it might be a long time from now.'

'The day after the day after tomorrow, Mak?'

'Well, perhaps the day after the day after the day after tomorrow.'

Ah OK, so a long long time from now...

All of a sudden. I want to sit next to Tante Lan again.

I want to hear her croaky low voice. I want to see her eyes disappear when she laughs. I want to see her beautiful long straight hair that hangs like rainfall.

'Oh!' I suddenly remember Puff. 'Poor little thing. He must get lonely when Tante Lan is away for a long time. Right, Mak?'

'Yes, I'm sure he misses her. But hold a moment… look at this… Here's a present for you from Tante Lan,' says Mak, handing me a bag made of polka-dot cloth – white spots on a green background – and tied up with yellow ribbon. The bag is a very wonky shape: it bulges at the top and to one side and at its base. Inside the bag sits something that looks a bit like a doll. His body is all stripy like a gethuk lindri (a famous sort of Javanese cake that's covered in stripes). Other bits of him are dark brown and he wears a green shirt with wooden buttons, just like Pak's rain coat. His arms are wide open. His feet too. His ears are gently rounded and stick out on either side of his head. He has two round eyes, as shiny as black marbles. His smiling mouth is stitched out of black thread.

'Now, Tante Lan told me this doll is a teddybear,' says Mak.

'A teddybear, Mak?'

'T-E-D-D-Y-B-E-A-R.'

I decide to write the bear's name on the top of a bit of old newspaper and show it to Mak.

'Mak, his name is going to be…'

'Teddy Bea?'

'Teddy *Bear*.'

'But you've written 'Teddy Bea' – where's the R at the end?'

Oh drat… I forgot about the R.

'Well, Teddy Bea sounds like a good name to me,' says Mak. 'Good afternoon, Teddy Bea.'

* Bea(r)

'Good afternoon, Mak!' I move Teddy Bea's hand to wave at Mak.

When I hold and kiss him, he smells of tobacco.

The same smell as Tante Lan.

89

Circus

Why oh why do I have to take naps?

I hate taking naps.

When I take a nap, I miss out on playing with Farida and I can't fly kites with Dul and Bud or ride Poni or play with Very Tiny Yellow Chick (who, to be honest, isn't really still a chick these days).

'So you won't be taking a nap then, Willa? Ahhh, that's fine. It just means that you'll be staying home with Mbok this evening. Does that sound OK by you?' says Mak.

What? Pak and Mak are going out? Of *course* I want to go with them. I don't want to stay here with Mbok, of this I am very sure.

'Where are we going, Mak?'

'I'm not sure, but Pak still has the car he borrowed so I imagine it'll be somewhere a decent way off. Pak said we're going to watch some sort of show that will be very funny.'

A funny show… What's that going to be?

Is it Kuda Kepang? Kuda Kepang is a sort of dance where men ride about on wooden hobby horses.

'I don't think so. But if you carry on refusing to have a nap, I guess it'll just be me and Pak going.'

Oh! Oh oh oh oh! You can't do this to me, Mak. I want to come with you. I absolutely *have* to.

'I'll go to bed right away, Mak. I'll get to sleep as fast as I can.'

I run to my room and jump onto the bed.

'How about washing your feet first, Willa? Your feet are absolutely filthy!' Mak pulls me off the bed. Yes Mak, of course I'll wash my feet and wash my face and wash my hands and change my clothes and go straight to sleep.

But I can't sleep. My eyes just won't stay closed. Whenever I shut them, I picture Kuda Kepang and Reog* and the sort of dancing I've seen at Farida's house. But Mak said it won't be like any of these sorts of shows. So what is it I'm going to see this evening with Mak and Pak?

Hey! That's Pak's voice. He's home already.

I can hear Mak telling Pak that I'm still napping.

I hear her come into my room.It's important that Mak thinks I actually took a proper nap. She sits down on the bed beside me.

'Willa, wake up, please. Pak is already home,' she whispers.

Ha, this I know...

'We're getting ready to go.'

This I know too.

Quick as a flash I jump out of bed. Pak is in the living room, sitting and smoking.

'Are we going out, Pak?'

'Yes we are. We're going to Taman Sari to see the circus, Willa.'

'What's the circus, Pak?'

'The circus is... well, it's a very interesting sort of show. There'll be men and women doing acrobatics, walking on a tightrope, riding unicycles and leaping into the air and there'll be a clown too...'

Acrobatics? Whenever I roll around on the bed, Mak says: *No more acrobatics thank you very much or you'll break*

---

* Reog – a traditional dance from East Java

the bed. So tonight I'm going to watch people rolling around on a bed? And a unicycle? And people walking along a rope?

'I love the circus and I think you and Mak are going to love it too. And what's more, this circus troupe is particularly impressive – they have come all the way from Germany. There'll be so many things to look at. You'll see for yourself.'

It sounds like the circus is really going to be *something*. I have the fastest shower ever.

And so we drive out to Tambaksari football field in the car Pak's borrowed from the office. By the time we arrive it's already starting to get dark. There are lots of people there and loudspeakers are booming with music, playing songs I've never heard before but which make me excited to watch the show.

'Look, there's the big stage where the performers will be.' Pak is pointing at a giant square right in the middle of the playing field.

There are all these bright lights zipping and zooming up and down and around us. We don't sit on the seats that are round the edge of the field. Instead, we sit down on a patch of grass nearer the stage.

'It's more comfortable to watch from here. The closer the better – so Willa can see everything clearly. Right, Mak?' says Pak. There are lots of other people sitting on the grass too. Some of them are even lying down.

All sorts of people keep on arriving and the grass, which was pretty much empty moments before, is suddenly packed.

Pak has been sitting with legs straight out in front of him, but he now has to cross them. Mak does the same.

When the sky gets dark, the lamps are finally lit and the music for the show starts. It's so loud I leap about a foot in the air in shock. It feels like something exploding deep inside my ears.

On stage, under these incredibly bright lights, four men with round noses, round hats and funny crooked legs start walking to and fro. They jump around then bump into one another and bounce up and down, before bumping into one another again. Everyone laughs: Pak, Mak and me too. 'Now these,' says Pak, 'are the clowns.'

Once the clowns have finished jumping all over the place, two dancers – a woman and a man – appear at the edge of the stage. All of a sudden the woman leaps up and the man catches her, then he throws her into the air and catches her again. Next, he takes her by one hand and she spins round like a propeller. Mak, Pak and I clap and clap and clap. How is she able to do this?

I'm all set to ask Mak when these two dancers are replaced by a great long line of women wearing tall feathery hats and tights with lots of holes in them. They dance together, kicking their legs into the air in perfect time.

'Any moment now they're going to start doing acrobatics, Willa,' whispers Pak, who has his arm round me.

Acrobatics?

'But where's the bed, Pak?'

Pak grins and shakes his head.

'There aren't any beds at the circus: they use a big safety net instead. Can you see it, over there, the net that looks like the enormous black mosquito net? That's what they use, instead of a bed.'

Oh *right*.

Next up, the ladies in the feathery hats start climbing a big rope ladder. At the top of the ladder, there's a little square platform where they all gather together before, one by one, they begin walking along a rope. They walk in a line, lifting their legs together – right, left, right, left – and then they run forwards and backwards, dancing away on this tiny rope suspended from one end of the stage to the other.

The dancers are still dancing on the tightrope when another member of the troupe rolls onto the rope riding on a unicycle. Something in my knees goes icy cold. And while this unicycle rolls back and forth on the rope, far below a man on the stage starts tossing things like bottles and oranges up to the performer on the unicycle. He catches every single one: he doesn't drop or fumble a thing. And while we're watching this, a woman with long hair appears with a rope tied round her forehead. Another performer comes and pulls the rope and ties it onto a short pole. The woman is then gradually pulled onto the top of the pole, and from there starts spinning her body round and round. Mak keeps holding her breath. 'What if the rope comes loose from her head?' she murmurs.

While I'm watching this lady balancing on the pole, Pak points to *another* rope ladder in a different part of the stage.

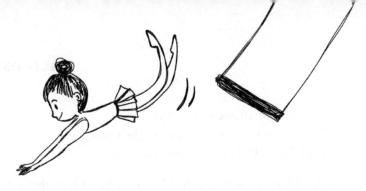

Here, there are performers hanging from little seats that swing back and forth across the stage. They jump and swap places without once crashing into one another or falling down. In fact, they make it look weirdly easy.

I can't remember how long I've been sitting on the grass in this field anymore – I guess because we've seen so many amazing things. After what still seems like no time at all, the performers line up on stage, including those women in the feathery hats. I clap my hands and Mak waves. Pak suggests we get closer to the stage and when we're near enough to see, I spot that all the circus performers have pale skin and long noses. Each and every one of them.

This is the very first time I've ever seen noses as long or skin as pale as this. I wave at them all and they wave right back at me. I feel pretty happy.

Pak says he can carry me if I'm feeling too tired to walk to the car. But I don't need any help. All I want to do is run and jump. I want to be a circus performer! I want to leap about and spin round and round and round…

On the way home, just before I fall asleep, I tell Mak that when I grow up, I want to join the circus.

Mak just says: 'Hmmm…'

Acrobat

Today I'm not allowed to go out.

I'm not even allowed to play in the house.

And I heard Mak tell Farida to go home.

Today I have to help Mbok tidy up my bed. Once the bed looks neat enough, I have to read a book that doesn't have ANY pictures in it. And I have to keep going until I finish it.

Mak is raging because I transformed the nice neat bed that Mbok had made into something that looks like it's been hit by a typhoon. All the pillows are now on the floor. The bolsters are under the bed. The sheets have all come loose. The metal hoop and pole that fixes onto the bed to hold my mosquito net is all bent out of shape. Before this happened to the bed, I also knocked Poni upside down. And because of all this, it's only right that I should be punished. Or that's what Mak says.

The thing is, all I wanted to do was play at being an acrobat. Just a little bit. Just to be like those ladies with the feathery hats last night. That's why I tried to stand on Poni's back. I was being so careful, but Poni started wobbling and then toppled over. And I fell on the floor as well. But I didn't get hurt, which was a win. The only casuality was Poni's left ear. And even that was only broken a *bit*. But anyway, after all this I wanted to keep practising my circus moves, so I headed to my bed. I did some swinging on it, hanging from the mosquito net's frame. And then I did a spot of somersault training on Mak's big bed.

Apparently none of this is allowed. Mak says that beds are *not* circus stages and *not* somewhere to jump about on or practise somersaults or swing from. But if this is the case, I put it to you: where and how is a person supposed to practise their acrobatics?

Because the thing is, I really do have to practise if I'm going to join the circus when I grow up. Which is exactly what I told Mak last night on the way home.

I think Mak must have already forgotten.

Motorbike

Yesterday afternoon, after I'd had my shower, I was sitting with Mak out on the terrace waiting for Pak to get home. And suddenly I heard this tremendously loud noise that went *brum-brum-brum-dum-dum-duuuuum…*

I leapt up and ran to the gate. Oh, it was Pak. And this was the sound of a motorbike!

The closer he got to the house, the louder the noise grew. Pak was grinning as he started to slow the motorbike down. He looked awesome riding on it. In no time at all, Dul had already come out to see it. He started stroking the motorbike while Pak chuckled.

'Do you want to have a go on it by any chance, Dul?' asked Pak.

Dul started nodding his head furiously.

'I want a go, Pak,' I said, 'Can I can I can I, Mak?' Mak was standing by the gate. She wasn't smiling and her eyebrows were all knotted up.

'And what's this?' Mak asked Pak in a weird flat voice.

'A motorbike, Marie,' said Pak, patting the handlebars. 'It's our motorbike. I picked one with a sidecar for you and Willa to sit in so, we don't have to borrow a car anymore if we want to go somewhere further away.'

'Oh, so you've bought it, have you?' asked Mak again. Her voice still sounded all flat. Her eyebrows were still knotted together.

'I'm going to buy it, yes. At the moment it belongs to Koh Sie's older brother. He's just got a new one. But before

I pay for it, I wanted to bring it home so we could try it out. So, what do you think? Great, isn't it?'

'Hmmm.' Mak just hummed. She nodded her head and went straight into the house. Her eyebrows were still all knotted together.

I saw that Pak's smile had disappeared. Only Dul was still laughing as he tried to get into the sidecar by holding onto our fence. He let his walking stick fall into the gutter, and once he'd climbed in he grabbed my hand and said 'Willa! Come in too! Come on!'

I couldn't help noticing just how miserable Pak's face now looked.

What happened?

But I still really wanted to have a go on the motorbike, so I climbed carefully into the sidecar and sat down next to Dul.

It felt excellent in there. There wasn't a whole lot of space, but all the same it wasn't too cramped.

The roar of the motorbike's engine made my whole body tremble. Dul laughed even harder, his hand patting the wall of the sidecar. But Pak didn't get the motorbike moving. Why? Had he forgotten he'd asked me and Dul to go on a drive with him.

'Pak, come on. Pak!' I reminded him.

'What? Where to?' Ah, he really had forgotten.

'Out on a ride. Anywhere!'

'A ride?'

'Yes! With Dul!'

'Okay, with Dul.'

Oh, hold on: where's Farida?

But the moment I started looking round for her, the motorcycle began to move. Dul started yelping and waving his arms around. Bud ran after us. He definitely wanted to come too, but the sidecar was too small for him or Farida to fit inside as well.

The motorcycle started moving very slowly, but the noise it made was still very loud. *Brum-brum-brum-dum-dum-duuuuum…*

One by one, our neighbours came out to see what was going on. Wow, it was serious fun. Pak drove us round alley numbers 11, 12 and 13, then he took us back home.

'Ah but that was too short, we need to go further,' Dul whispered as the motorbike pulled up at our house again.

Yep, he was right. It would have better to go even further. But it was almost dark and I wondered if perhaps Mak wanted to have a go on the motorbike. Perhaps her eyebrows wouldn't be all knotted up in the middle any more if she had a ride on it.

Pak pushed the motorbike through the gate into our yard and parked it under the pine tree.

'Can I just sit here in the sidecar, Pak?' I asked.

'Sure, but be careful, alright?'

I went and got Atik, Teddy Bea and Gorilla to come and ride with me in Pak's motorbike.

Ah! It was good in there… I crossed my legs a bit and leant back like I was in an extremely comfy chair.

Suddenly, Mak was standing next to the motorbike. She had her arms folded tightly across her chest.

'Get out of this motorbike right away. It's no place to play,' she said. Seeing the look on Mak's face, I knew I'd

have to climb out of it as quick as I could, taking Atik,
Teddy Bea and Gorilla with me.

'But can I ride it tomorrow, Mak? And can we go to
school in the motorbike?'

'Let's see about tomorrow,' said Mak, nudging me back
towards the house.

Ah, but it would be so good to go to school in the motorbike. Brum-brum-brum-dum-dum-duuuuum…

So here we are this morning and I'm all ready to go to school with Pak. I sit in the sidecar of his motorbike. I spy that Dul, Farida, Bud and all the neighbours are watching the motorbike closely. Maybe it's because they like it so much? Mak says I have to hold on tight to the handle in the sidecar.

Before we leave, Mak asks Pak: 'Can you please make it a bit less noisy?'

'Less noisy? I'm afraid I can't. That's just the sound it makes,' says Pak.

And off we go.

Brum-brum-brum-dum-dum-duuuuum…

The noise of the motorbike makes everything shake: the window frames, my whole body… The distance between our house and the school shrinks to almost nothing in the motorbike. When we pull up to the school, all my classmates and the teacher are all standing by the gates. Everyone wants to see Pak's motorbike. *Brum-brum-brum-dum-dum-duuuuum…*

I assume that we're going to ride to school on Pak's motorbike every day from now on. But in the end we only keep the motorbike for two days. Pak takes it back to Oom Sie. He tells him the that the motorbike was too noisy for our neighbours.

'Mak wants a motorbike with a gentler sound so it won't frighten the neighbours when we run the engine,' says Pak.

A ha. Every time we turned on the engine, the noise sent the neighbours leaping out of their houses. I thought it was just because they wanted to see Pak's motorbike. But yes, maybe it was actually because the engine was just way too noisy.

So Pak returns the motorbike and sidecar to Oom Sie.

Then a week later, Pak comes home with a much smaller motorcycle. When Pak arrives with this little motorbike, Mak gives him this huge smile. Pak says it's not a real motorbike, but it's actually a scooter. It's called a Vespa. And the noise it makes sounds like this: *tung-tung-tung-tung.*

And Mak is much happier.

The lady with the pointy nose

A couple of days ago, while Mbok was ironing the clothes, she started telling Mak (who was busy reading a brand-new magazine) that somebody's bought Pak Wardiman's old house. It's all been renovated and the new owners are going to move in soon. Mbok said the new owners have already been to look round several times. Mbok said they look like they're from India.

'Oh? How do you know, Mbok?'

'*Everybody* knows, Nyah,' says Mbok.

And then yesterday Dul and Farida came and told me that there's a new boy living in this house who's the same age as Dul.

Dul said, 'He looked like he wanted to play with me, but his mum said he had to clean the yard.'

And then Farida said the boy had been holding a broom and dustpan made from part of an old oil can. But they *didn't* say that these new neighbours were from India. What are the Indian people like?

'When they've moved in properly, we can visit them. With neighbours, it's important that we look after one another,' says Mak, still reading her magazine.

'Will we get to visit their house, Mak?'

'Yes, we'll visit them so we can make friends with them,' says Mak.

'Can we bring Farida with us when we visit the new neighbours, Mak?'

'Of course. Perhaps Farida's mother would like to come along too. I'll ask her later.'

This is all very exciting.

The next day, when I get home from school, I deliberately walk very slowly down the alley. Who knows, maybe I'll get to meet the little boy who Dul and Farida told me about. But nobody appears. Even though I can see a motorbike parked in their yard. I stop for a moment by their gate. Maybe the little boy will be playing outside or sweeping the ground again.

And then suddenly the front door opens. I jump in surprise. In front of me stands a lady wearing what looks like a sort of bedspread wrapped round her body. Her hair is tied up at the top of her head. Her eyebrows are black and curved like an upside down U. And there between the two arches of her eyebrows is a little red dot. It's as red as Mak's lipstick.

'What's your name?' The lady with the lipstick dot on her forehead is walking towards me. I answer, but perhaps my voice is too quiet because she asks me again. Now she's standing right in front of me. She's smiling warmly and I see that her teeth are bright white.

'Willa. Na Willa,' I say in a bigger voice, while I carry on looking closely at her face. She has a pointy nose. I think to myself: I've definitely seen a nose like this before. But where was it? Ah yes... it was at the German circus.

And now, standing behind the lady in the bedspread, here is a boy about the same height as Dul. A *ha*, this must be the person Farida told me about.

'Willa, this is Karuna. It would be lovely if you might

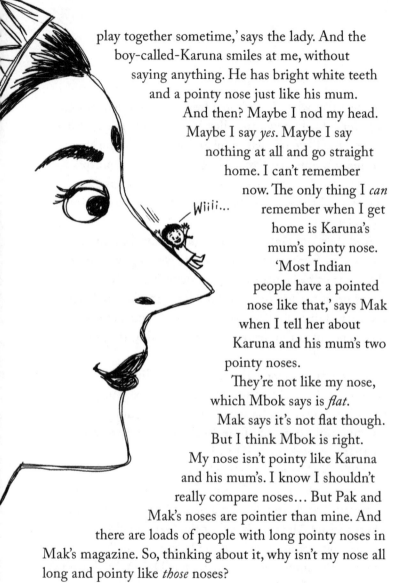

play together sometime,' says the lady. And the
boy-called-Karuna smiles at me, without
saying anything. He has bright white teeth
and a pointy nose just like his mum.
And then? Maybe I nod my head.
Maybe I say *yes*. Maybe I say
nothing at all and go straight
home. I can't remember
now. The only thing I *can*
remember when I get
home is Karuna's
mum's pointy nose.
'Most Indian
people have a pointed
nose like that,' says Mak
when I tell her about
Karuna and his mum's two
pointy noses.
They're not like my nose,
which Mbok says is *flat*.
Mak says it's not flat though.
But I think Mbok is right.
My nose isn't pointy like Karuna
and his mum's. I know I shouldn't
really compare noses... But Pak and
Mak's noses are pointier than mine. And
there are loads of people with long pointy noses in
Mak's magazine. So, thinking about it, why isn't my nose all
long and pointy like *those* noses?
Perhaps, if I pull at the end of my nose like *this*, it'll

Wiiii...

start looking like the noses of all the performers in the German circus. Or like Karuna's mum's nose. Or like the people in Mak's magazine.

But when I let go of my nose it just goes back to normal.

I don't like my nose.

I tell Mak that I want a nose that's long and pointy. Mak tells me that as I get older, my nose will gradually get longer and pointier.

'Just like the Indian lady, Mak?'

'Her name is Ibu Rao, Willa.'

Oh! So Mak already knows Karuna's mum's name.

'OK… just like Ibu Rao, Mak?'

'Well, perhaps not quite as long as that. But it'll be more like Mak and Pak's noses.'

'Why?'

'Because you're Mak and Pak's daughter. So your eyes, your nose, your hair: they are all just like Mak and Pak's. You're not Ibu Rao's daughter. You're not Karuna's sister. And you're not from India.'

'Hmmm…'

If it can't have a nose like Karuna or his mum, then why isn't my nose like Pak and Mak's *now*? I don't want to have a really pointy nose – I just want it to be a bit pointier? Just a little. Maybe I should pull the end of my nose every day. In fact, I really ought to get to work on this right away, so it can grow as quickly as possible. Yes. So if you don't mind, please excuse me while I start pulling at the end of my nose.

Nose #1

'Why are you pulling at your nose, Willa?'

After I've had my shower and got all ready for school, Mbok sees me pulling at the end of my nose.

'Stop it.'

She asks me to take my hand off my nose because it'll take me ages to get dressed using just the other hand.

'Why are you pulling at your nose, Willa?' asks Mak as we eat breakfast.

'I want my nose to get pointier.'

'Ohhh, so you want to have a pointy nose, do you? Listen, if you were born with a flat little nose then you'll always have a flat little nose,' says Mbok, laughing like a drain.

I don't like it when Mbok laughs like this.

Mak pries my fingers off my nose. 'Stop it, Willa. Yes, your nose will grow and get pointier at some point. Come on: stop it. You shouldn't pull at it like that. Eat up or you're going to be late for school.'

My hands are removed from my nose.

On the way to school, I have another go at my nose.

Mak clears her throat. I leave my nose alone.

I pull it again and Mak clears her throat again.

I leave it alone again.

When we get to the last turning before school, Mak stops. She holds my hands and crouches down in front of me.

'Willa, please stop pulling at your nose. Come on. Walk sensibly, we're nearly at school now.' Mak's voice is getting louder.

I nod my head quickly. 'Yes Mak.'

'Mak doesn't want to see these fingers pulling at your nose anymore. Let your nose grow by itself and let it get a bit pointier in the normal way.'

'But… can I pull it tomorrow?'

'Your nose isn't going to grow overnight, Willa. It'll take many years and it'll grow by itself. Be patient. So no more nose-pulling today or tomorrow, OK? Do you understand, Willa?' Mak asks.

I nod again. Mak is holding my hand. We walk into school and as we arrive, Ibu Juwita is ringing the bell. Mak sets off for home.

While I wait in line, I pull at my nose again.

Just a little bit.

Nose #2

Mak picks me up to go home. Just like usual.

But then something unusual happens. Bu Juwita asks Mak to come to her office. I have to wait outside.

After not so long, Mak comes out.

Her forehead is all crinkly. Her eyebrows are knotted into one.

Eugh. What's wrong?

All the way home on the bicycle, Mak is silent.

My heart beats faster and faster. It feels like it's trying to jump out of my chest.

When we get home, Mak directs me to sit down in my little wicker chair.

'Willa, do you remember what I said about your nose?'

Oh.

'That I'm not allowed to pull it?'

'So, why did you pull your nose all day at school?'

This is… not good.

'Yes, Mak…'

'Yes Mak? Yes Mak *what*?'

Um…

'Yes Mak, I forgot and I did pull my nose. Several times.'

'Even when Bu Guru said DON'T DO THAT?'

Heck.

'Yes Mak…'

'And then, when you were in the playground, you found a clothes peg and used *that* to pull at your nose?'

Ach. Ibu Guru is officially a tell-tale. Just like Mbok.
I really don't like this.

'Well, she told me that I needed my hand to write and draw with. But I wanted to pull my nose at the same time. So I...'

'And when your teacher took that peg off your nose you went berserk because it was so painful.'

The thing is, yes, I did scream. A lot. But only because I didn't want her to take the peg off my nose. Not because it *hurt*.

Mak takes a very long and very deep breath. Then she scratches her head. And then she shakes her head.

'Willaaaaa... You get the shape of your nose from me and from Pak. When you get older, your nose will grow longer and it might well get a bit pointier too. Like mine and your father's. But it's never going to be as pointy as Ibu Rao's nose because...'

'Because I'm not Ibu Rao's daughter.'

'Exactly. So you don't need to pull at it or to put a clothes peg on it ever again. This nose of yours will grow all by itself.'

'But there's still such a long time left to go, Mak.'

'Yes, it grows little by little. Until it's bigger.'

So this means a long time. A really long time. A really really really really really really long time.

That evening, Pak almost chokes when Mak tells him about me and my nose and the clothes peg.

'See, Pak!' I show Pak how with just one careful tug I can make my nose longer and pointier. Pak pulls my hand off my nose.

'Why are you so set on having a nose like those German circus performers or someone from India?'

'Mbok says my nose is all small and flat.'

'Oh, Mbok said that? She doesn't know *how* your nose is going to grow.'

'But I'm going to have to wait such a long time, Pak…'

Pak takes a deep breath. Mak does too, another big one.

'Listen to me. When I was little, my nose certainly wasn't as pointy as it is now. But the bigger I got, the pointier my nose grew. Same as Mak's nose,' explains Pak while touching Mak's nose.

'Is this true, Mak?'

Mak nods her head. Vigorously.

'And Mak's nose is plenty pointy enough, right?' Pak asks me.

Yes. It is. And Pak's nose is too.

'Well, as you grow older, your nose will be just like Mak's nose. How about that? It's perfect, right?'

'But I want my nose to be like yours, Pak,'

'Ah, but that's even easier, because *this* nose is actually smaller than Mak's,' says Pak, tapping his own nose.

Even easier?

'And your nose will grow all by itself. You really don't need to put a clothes peg on it,' says Mak.

Should I pull on it?

'There's no need to do that either.'

Alright, alright, I won't tug at my nose anymore.

Promise.

But in bed, once the lights have been turned off, I give my nose a pull.

Just a little one.

For a moment.

And only so it might get pointy just that little bit quicker.

At the harbour

In the afternoons, if Pak gets home early enough and Oom Sie isn't visiting us, Pak loves taking me and Mak on the scooter to Tanjung Perak harbour for a stroll. Mak always brings a little stack of tins filled with chicken or some soup. Mak says that if we get hungry, we can just eat the food we brought from home. There's really no need to buy anything. And I always bring my water bottle that I take to school every day.

At the harbour, Pak and Mak usually suggest I wander round the port. Sometimes Mak brings a novel to read when we arrive and sit down. Pak likes bringing a notebook plus a pen or pencil. He loves drawing the people and the boats in the port.

If Mak isn't feeling very well or has too much to do, then just me and Pak go to the harbour. When Mak's not here with us, Pak will sit down on the bench alone, smoking and drawing. If he gets bored with his drawing, he'll lay down on the bench and sometimes fall asleep there.

I'm allowed to walk by myself here: I've no need for anyone to come with me. I know I'm not allowed to go too close to the edge of the harbour. And I don't quite know why, but every time I get close to the edge, I feel the ocean calling me to jump in.

This afternoon though, Pak doesn't bring his notebook and pencil with him. While Pak smokes, he talks to Mak *privately*. Pak tells me that he and Mak need to talk about *grown-up things* and so they ask me to wander round on my own for a little while. I love the harbour. I never get bored of watching the boats. But all the same, my number one favourite thing in the whole world is to listen to Mak when she talks.

Visiting the new neighbours

Mak and Farida's mum are going to visit Ibu Rao's house. Farida and I are going along too. Mak is bringing chicken fritters and Farida's mum is bringing palm sugar fritters.

Ibu Rao is wearing the same piece of cloth all twisted round her, and between her eyebrows is a little dot as red as Mak's lipstick.

Farida's mum and Mak tell her all about the history of our alleyway (which is called Gang Krembangan) and about who lives next-door and opposite to her. Ibu Rao then tells them all about where she used to live in Jakarta. And then they do a lot of laughing together.

Farida and I start getting to know Karuna. It seems like he doesn't have all that many toys. Or perhaps his toys are tidied away in drawers somewhere in his room. Then again, Karuna has a gazillion books. In the living room, there's a little bookshelf absolutely crammed with books. He lets me and Farida pick out some books and then we sit together right by the bookcase. We read. We do not chat.

On the table, Mrs. Rao has set out glasses filled with cold water and sweet red syrup called frambozen, and there is a jar of crackers which are like the sort of crackers we usually have (called karak) but even thinner. Karuna takes one for himself. Cerrrrr-unch. The noise of his chewing makes me hungry. Farida's mum takes one and splits it in two: half for her, half for Farida. Mak does the same, so I get half a cracker.

The thing is though, I actually wanted to do the same as Karuna: I wanted to take a really big cracker and have it all to myself. I didn't want to share that cracker with another soul.

So Farida and I start eating our crackers and oh – oh! – OH! Yuk, what is this? It tastes completely different from normal crackers. It doesn't taste of shrimp like they usually do. It tastes more like, well, like jamu.*

Eugh...

Well, I suppose I was lucky only to get half a cracker after all. If I'd had a whole one, I really don't know how I'd have ever managed to finish it. Farida's face is looking pretty put-out about the taste of her cracker too. We pick up our glasses and gulp down the red syrupy drink hoping the taste of those crackers will be banished for EVER.

'Karuna, what sort of cracker is this?' Farida asks Karuna, who's reading a book while nibbling on a cracker.

'It's a poppadum. It's tasty, right? Do you want another one?'

Quick as a flash, Farida and I shake our heads.

---

* jamu – traditional Indonesian herbal medicine made of things like roots, bark, flowers, seeds, leaves and fruits

Back and forth, to and fro

Pak has gone to Jakarta again.

And this time he's gone longer than ever.

Mak says Pak has lots of work to do there. She says he'll come home as soon as he's finished. But when will this be?

Mak has no idea.

Sigh. It feels like Pak's been gone for absolutely ages. Every day on the way home from school, I imagine that perhaps Pak has come home. But then when I get home, Pak's not there. Every single night I ask Mak when he'll come back but Mak just says she doesn't know. *Maybe tomorrow.* She keeps saying this same old thing. But tomorrow comes. And then the day after tomorrow and the day after the day after tomorrow but still Pak isn't home.

Finally I stop asking.

Then this Saturday morning I wake up and smell that familiar scent: tobacco. Pak must have come back! I pull open the mosquito net and leap out of bed. And there in the living room is Pak, sitting and smoking.

'Good morning!' says Pak when he sees me. He hugs me so tight with his big arms that I almost can't breathe. 'How are you doing, Willa? What are you going to tell me all about?'

When I was waiting for Pak to get home, I had a million things all ready to tell Pak. But now he's here, sitting in front of me, I lose all my words.

I spy a tin of corned beef on the table for Mak and wonder what he might have bought for me. There's no parcel or pile of new books on the table for me. I start thinking that perhaps Pak hasn't brought anything for me....

'Hey, come and have a look at this, Willa,' says Pak as he opens up a big brown leather bag. Pak takes out a wooden box. On the lid, written in red, it says: *Goldilocks and the Three Bears* and then there are some other words that I can't read. Those words must be written in English. Pak slides the lid off the wooden box. Inside there are lots and lots of little coloured cubes.

'It's a wooden puzzle. If you rearrange these pieces, you'll find it makes a picture of a little girl called Goldilocks who one day meets Daddy Bear, Mummy Bear and Baby Bear. Would you like to have a go, Willa?' Pak hands me the big square box.

'How about you play with your Goldilocks puzzle *after* school? It's time to go to school now,' says Mak, taking the box from my hands.

Eugh. School!

'How about I stay at home today? It's been a long time since we chatted and drew pictures together, right Willa?'

Yes yes YES.

'A day off? Do you mean playing truant from school?' asks Mak in a high-pitched voice. A ha, *that* voice. I quickly turn and face Pak. I have no desire to see Mak's eyebrows all knotted together.

'Oh she can miss one day. How much can happen at school in just a day? Yes, Willa?' says Pak, catching my eye.

I would be so very happy to stay at home today.

'Of course she can't. She can't just skip school like that.'

Mak's voice hasn't gone back to normal yet.

I really want to stay at home and miss school and make that special picture with the little wooden cubes. But perhaps it's a good idea for me to go to school so Mak's eyebrows can return to their usual shape.

'Come and have a shower, Willa.' Mbok is calling me.

I race to the bathroom. When I finish washing, Mak is waiting for me to come and eat my breakfast and take my vitamins and fish oil. I note my water bottle is filled up and ready to go. Yep, I'm going to school.

'You're still going to school today, OK?' says Mak. 'Pak will take you.' A ha, so I'm going to school with Pak. So I can still chat to him and he can still whistle and sing to me in English. While I put on my shoes, I hear the scooter engine being turned on: *tung-trung-tung-tung-trung...*

Let's go, Pak.

And see you later, Goldilocks and the three bears.

Top secret

Pak picks me up from school.

But before we get home, Pak turns the scooter to take us to the ice cream shop near church. Pak and I eat ice cream cones, sitting on wooden chairs inside the shop.

'Willa, this is our secret, alright? Please don't tell Mak that we had an ice cream,' says Pak as he pays.

'Why's that, Pak?'

'Mak doesn't really like it if we have ice cream before lunch,' says Pak, looking me straight in the eye. 'Don't tell Mak. OK?'

Oh.

My heart beats faster.

What if Mak finds out? If I don't tell her anything about the ice cream, Mak surely won't find out. So I just have to not tell her. But what if I forget that I can't tell her?

Oh.

I have to try and remember not to tell Mak.

When I get home, I try and solve the cubes puzzle, arranging the pieces so I can see that excellent drawing of the three bears and the little girl. I sit next to Pak as he tells me about his time in Jakarta.

He tells me about the night market there and how it's so much bigger and busier than the markets here, and with lots more toys too. There are so many more shows for children that he thinks I'd love to watch in Jakarta.

Sometime.
Someday.

That night, as I close my mosquito net, I tell Mak that I
want Pak to take me to school on Monday.

'Uh? Why's that?'

'Because then I can eat ice cream, Mak.'

DRAT.

An announcement

This afternoon we go to the harbour again.

On the way home, we stop off at the ice cream shop.

Maybe this is to help stop Mak feeling so cross that Pak and I had ice cream without her before lunchtime.

I still can't believe I managed to forget to keep mine and Pak's ice cream secret. AHHG.

Pak and I have the same flavour of bright yellow ice cream in our cones. I lick it as quick as I can so it doesn't melt and make my hands all sticky or make the cone all soggy and gross.

Pak orders Mak a bowl of white ice cream with raisins floating about in it, which she eats in slow, tiny spoonfuls. Mak's eyes close every time she eats some. Ah, it looks properly delicious. When we come here next, I'd like to get the same flavour as Mak.

When Mak has got halfway through her bowl of ice cream, Pak moves his chair closer to both of us and holds our hands.

'Mak, Willa… Pak has something to tell you…' he whispers. He's smiling so much that his eyes have disappeared. Mak leans her head forward until it almost touches Pak's.

'What's that?' Mak is whispering as well.

'We're going to move to Jakarta,' says Pak.

Now his eyes are wide open.

I hear Mak take a deep breath.

She doesn't say a word.

'Move to Jakarta?'

'Yes, we're going to move to Jakarta. We're going to live there.'

Mak is suddenly sitting bolt upright. She stops eating her ice cream.

'When?'

'Soon,' says Pak, gripping Mak's hands tight. Her head, that she'd leant forward to touch Pak's, is now back in its usual position. She is sitting up straight, her back set against the back of the chair. Her forehead is all wrinkled up.

'This afternoon?'

'Oh, not that fast, Willa. We have so much to get ready. Right, Mak? I hope it'll be two weeks from now. Or maybe three weeks. At the latest it'll be one month until we go,' says Pak.

Mak is still silent. Her hands – that Pak had been holding onto – are now folded over her chest.

'And when we've finished visiting Jakarta, will we come back here?'

'I don't think so,' says Pak.

But if I'm not coming back, how will I see Dul and Farida and Bud?

'Can Farida come with us?'

'That's not possible, I'm afraid.'

'Why, Pak?'

'Because Farida's mum and dad are here. If she came with us, her mum and dad would be so sad.'

'OK, then how about Farida plus her mum and her dad come with us?'

'Farida isn't coming with us, Willa, and neither are her parents,' says Pak.

'Dul, Bud, Ibu Juwita…'

'They can't come with us to Jakarta.'

But who am I going to play with there?

And what about school?

'You'll go a new school in Jakarta. There'll be new teachers, new friends,' says Pak again.

But I want Farida to come with me. I want the same school as TK Juwita, I want Ibu Juwita, Endang, Gatot…

I don't want to go to Jakarta.

'Willa, we're going to live in Jakarta and we won't come back here for a long time. But moving there is going to be brilliant. Because you'll have even more friends. So not just Farida, Dul, Bud and your classmates like Joko, Asih…'

'Sri, Sumi, Endang, Eko…'

'You'll make so many new friends. And you can write letters from Jakarta to all your friends here. You write so well, yes? So you can write letters and send postcards to Dul and Farida…'

Write letters and send postcards to Farida, Dul and Bud, telling them about Jakarta?

This I can do.

'I bet I can write a lot of things about Jakarta, Pak.'

'Oh, I bet you can!' says Pak. 'And Mak and Pak can help you write letters, if you'd like that.'

'I'll write them myself.'

'Good. Very good. This is excellent' says Pak, smiling so widely and handing Mak's ice cream to me. I eat it straight-away because it's already starting to melt and taste like milk.

On the way home, Mak is silent.

Pak is silent.

I'm silent too.

But what I really want to do is ask Pak about everything.

Discussion

Ida and I are playing kitchens round the side of our house, accompanied by Very Tiny Yellow Chick who's looking for worms.

'Last night I woke up and heard Mak and Pak talking.'

'Were they arguing?'

'Nope. They were having a discussion.'

'Were they speaking in loud voices?'

'Yes, a bit loud…'

'Well that's called arguing.'

'But they weren't angry. They just had slightly loud voices.'

'Because when people are arguing, they talk loudly. That's normal for parents. While the children sleep, they argue…'

I wonder if Farida is right, actually: were Mak and Pak arguing?

I don't want to believe it but I don't really know if they were just speaking loudly or having an actual argument.

And if they *were* arguing, what was it about? Moving to Jakarta?

Yes, perhaps that was the reason.

'Jakarta? Do you want to go? Will you be travelling round? Like when I went to Madura?'

'Pak said we're going live there, in our own house…'

'Your own house? In Jakarta? Wow, that means you really are moving to Jakarta. Hmmm. Is Jakarta far from here?'

'Pak says you have to go by plane or boat.'

'That means it's really far. Why do you have to go? Why don't you stay here? You can live at our house.'

'But I really want to be with Mak.'

I don't want Pak and Mak to go without me while I live with Farida. Mak has to be with me. I have to be with Mak.

'OK, so you and Mak can stay at my house. My house is pretty big, right?'

It's true. Farida's house *is* pretty big. I could sleep in her room. Or in the space by the prayer room. Or behind the house in Mbak Tini's room which is empty now.

'But do you think Pak will be happy with this?'

'Ahh, it'll be fine. I'll get my dad to talk to your dad.'

OK, so maybe this will work.

'When does your dad next go to Jakarta?'

Hmm, this I don't know. Maybe in two weeks. Or next month. I never really know when things are happening. I can't tell the difference between something a fortnight from now or a month away.

'But what if Pak doesn't want me and Mak to live at your house?'

'Hmmm… It's a good question… I guess it'll mean you really have to go to Jakarta.'

'I can write letters.' I remember Tante Lan's letters to Mak and Pak.

'Who to?'

'To you and Dul. And Bud too.'

'Bud can't read, so that's not going to work.'

'You'll have to read them to him.'

'Or maybe you should wait until when he's learnt how to read. But promise me you're coming back, yes?'

'Sure. I'll be back. But Pak said it wouldn't be for a while.'

'Please don't go for too long. Who am I am going to play dolls and kitchens with?'

I see the problem. Dul, Bud… they don't like playing dolls with me and Farida. And Mbak Tini is too big to play now. She's married so lives in Jember with her husband who has the gold teeth.

'Here's the thing. I'll let you go now, but then the day after the day after the day after tomorrow, you have to come back. OK?'

'The day after the day after the day after tomorrow?'

'Yes.'

'Okay. I'd better go home.'

'And there's no need for all this letter-writing. Just come back soon, right?' Farida carries on pretending to cook the hibiscus flowers.

I hear the sound of Pak's scooter coming round the corner. This means it's time for me to go and have a shower.

'Will you come to my house later for prayers?' asks Farida.

'Not today – I want to chat to Pak.'

'Sure.' And with that, Ida races home. She has to have a shower because prayers start at 6 o'clock.

After my shower, I'm all ready to sit out on the terrace. I wait for Pak

But it seems Pak hasn't finished talking to Mak yet.

Maybe I should go and remind *him* to go and have a shower.

As I approach the kitchen table, Mak stands up from her chair.

'Willa, how about going to Farida's house? You could go and pray with her.'

'But I want to listen to Pak and Mak's stories.'

'Maybe tomorrow night? Right now, Pak has so many things to do.'

'What sort of things, Mak?' Perhaps I can help.

'They're grown-up things,' says Mak, her lips all tense and flat. Not smiling like usual.

'Yes, Paul?' This is the very first time in the history of everything that Mak has called Pak by his first name. When Mak calls me by my full name it means I have to be careful because it's a sign that she's angry. So does this mean…?

'Go to Farida's house and pray with her.'

'Yes, Mak.'

I run to Farida's home and go into the big room. Farida is already on the first line. I take my place next to her, with the book in front of us. Farida is using the little pointing stick to read.

Right to left.

Right to left.

When Mak calls for me to come home, the sky is already full of stars.

Mak's eyes are all red.

Maybe something got caught in her eye. Dust.

Getting ready #1

Pak has gone back to Jakarta.

Mak says that Pak has lots and lots to organise.

The most important of all is the place we're going to live. He has to get all sorts of things ready in time for when Mak and I arrive.

At home, Mak is making this extremely long list of all the stuff we need to take with us to Jakarta.

I have a little box to put any toys and books in that I want to take. But this box is so small. A couple of books later and the box is basically full. I want to take ALL my books. But Mak says this is impossible. So I have to leave some of my books at Farida and Dul's houses. The same goes for my toys. Poni the wooden horse with the broken left ear... well, he's going to live at Bud's house.

'He'll be so happy there!' says Mak.

Bud is certainly pretty happy, Mak. But what if *I* want to ride on Poni again? Will I able to come back to Bud's house and get him back?

'There'll be toys just like Poni there. Do you remember when Pak told you how many more toyshops there are in Jakarta?'

Yep. This I do remember.

But Teddy Bea, Atik and Gorilla can all come with me. And the Goldilocks cubes.

Mak puts all her records in a big wooden box. Mak says they're going to Oom Sie's house. Everything is going to be stored there for a while.

Then when our house in Jakarta is all ready, that box

will be sent over.
Erres – the big
radio that makes
music – is going
to Oom Sie's
house too.

Lots of
Mak's books and
magazines are
now in a box
too, but Mak
says these are all
going to be given
to the church
library. Mak gave
some books to
Ibu Juwita too. Mak isn't bringing her crocodile-skin bag.
And her shoes with the pointy toes and high heels aren't
coming to Jakarta either. Mak says they'll use up too much
space in the suitcase.

Pans, plates, spoons, forks… none of these are coming
with us to Jakarta. Mak put them all into big bowls,
wrapped them in newspaper and tied them up with string.
She gave some to Farida's mum and there are some for
Bud's Mak and some for Mbok.

I really want Mbok to come with us but Mak says Mbok
has too many responsibilities in Tuban. So she can't go all
the way to Jakarta.

Mak picked me up from school this afternoon. And
now she's sitting in Ibu Juwita's office. All my friends have
already gone home.

After they have some sort of discussion, Ibu Juwita comes out and takes my hands.

'So Willa, you're going be a Jakarta kid,' she says.

I nod my head. My eyes feel all hot. Ibu Juwita leans down and gives me a huge hug. And then I really start crying. Ibu Juwita take a handkerchief out of her pocket. Mak squeezes my shoulders.

'Don't cry. With any luck we'll meet again one day, Willa,' says Ibu Juwita. 'And remember to keep on reading in your new home.'

I nod.

Mak shakes Ibu Juwita's hand.

I don't like crying but my eyes are full of tears again.

On the way home, Mak tells me that when I arrive in Jakarta, I'll make lots of new friends who'll make me happy. And that in Jakarta there'll be lots of teachers who will help me get cleverer and cleverer and that I'll learn all sorts of new things. English included.

The thing is, I want to make lots of new friends.

And I do want to get cleverer and learn lots of new things.

And I really want to be able to speak English.

But all the same, I'd still rather carry on learning here.

There's no need to go all that way to Jakarta.

So how about it, Mak? Staying here.

But I know Mak is going to say we can't.

My eyes feel hot all over again.

And now my nose is all full of water…

Getting ready #2

Pak came back from Jakarta two days ago.

As soon as he got home, Mak took Pak to look at all the stuff she'd sorted out.

After that, Pak and Mak carried on talking. And every time I went near them, Mak told me to help Mbok in the kitchen or feed the Very Tiny Yellow Chick (who, yes, is already a lot bigger) or just go and play with Farida.

I decided to play with Farida.

In other news, Very Tiny Yellow Chick is going to live at Dul's house.

Then when I get home this afternoon, I find Mak sitting out on the terrace. It looks like Mak and Pak have finally finished talking. Pak is sitting next to Mak, smoking. Pak's legs are all stretched out and he's leaning back, watching the cigarette rings he's blowing drift up to the sky.

'We're going to leave tomorrow afternoon, Willa,' says Mak.

I jump straight into Mak's lap.

'Tomorrow?'

Mak nods.

'Will we take the plane? And what about tickets?'

'Pak has bought them,' says Mak, 'and I took Teddy Bea and Gorilla out of the toy box so they can keep you company during the journey.'

'Do Teddy Bea and Gorilla need tickets too, Mak?'

'Oh no, they don't need tickets. You can just put them on your lap.'

I move across to sit on Pak's lap.

'Pak, can we go to the harbour in Jakarta, like we do here?'

'Of course, but perhaps not as often because the port's a bit further from our house there. A ha, but we can watch films because there's a cinema near where we're going to live.'

'Is there a school?'

'Oh there are lots of schools there! You can choose what sort of school you go to there…'

'Will there be lots of books at school?'

'Of course. I'm pretty sure all schools have lots of books.'

'And do you think I'm going to make new friends at school, Pak?'

'Ab-so-lutely. You're going to make lots and lots of new friends.'

'Will we have a radio at home, Pak?'

'Yes, but only a small one. Not as big as Erres. But we might have a television there too,' says Pak, raising his eyebrows.

'A television?'

'Yes, it's a box that you watch. All sorts of films and music come out of it,' says Pak.

Wow. I want to watch television right away.

'Will there be any windows in our house?'

'Yes, there'll be plenty of windows.'

'And will there be a fence?'

'Yes, one even taller than the one here.'

'And will there be a pine tree, Pak?'

'Hmmm… I should think so, yes.'

'And when we get to Jakarta, can I listen to Mak's record collection?'

'Hmmm… if Oom Sie has already sent them on to us that should be possible, yes.'

'And are we really leaving tomorrow, Pak?'

'Yes, Willa'

I slide down from Pak's lap and run to Farida's house. I race through the door without even knocking.

'Mak says I'm leaving tomorrow!'

Farida stands in the doorway. She doesn't say anything but her mouth starts moving. She looks like she wants to cry. Me too.

'But if you leave tomorrow then the day after the day after the day after tomorrow you have to come back, OK?'

'Yes, I'll be back the day after the day after the day after tomorrow. I will. I'll come back then.'

Farida takes my hand and we leave the house and ran to Dul's house. Farida is calling Dul's name the whole time until we get to his gate. Dul appears. He's so surprised he's forgotten to bring his walking stick.

'Willa is leaving tomorrow. Tomorrow!'

Dul stands still, holding onto the doorframe. He looks like he's thinking extremely hard about something. His mouth is set tight and his nose is all wrinkled up.

'But when are you coming back?' asks Dul.

'She'll be back the day after the day after the day after tomorrow,' answers Farida.

'But that's a long time!' Dul says.

'But I'll write you a letter, Dul!'

'And then I'll have to reply, will I? Huh!' He turns around and goes back into his house. Farida runs after him and I follow but Dul closes the door. Farida and I call out to him. We knock on the door. But Dul doesn't answer us.

And he keeps the door closed.

Mbok

I wake up in the middle of the night.

Maybe it's because I drank too much water before going to bed. I creep out of bed and tiptoe to the bathroom.

As I start to head back to my room, Mbok is there standing in front of the bathroom door. All of a sudden she hugs me. She is crying.

'When you're in Jakarta… be good, Willa,' she says, dabbing at her eyes.

I nod, but I can't say anything. I'm out of breath. And now I'm crying too.

'Mbok, please come with us to Jakarta.'

'I'm old, little one. In Jakarta, it'd only cause trouble for your mother and father,' Mbok whispers between sobs.

'But who will be there with me?'

'There'll be a new Mbok,' she says, patting my head.

Oh… now I'm crying again.

I don't want a new Mbok.

'When we go, will you stay here?'

'No, I'll go back to Tuban.'

Whenever there's a big festival, Mbok goes back to Tuban, where her niece lives. She has children now. Mbok doesn't have any children.

Mak told me that a long time ago Mbok's husband went to Surabaya where he said he was going to make lots of money, but instead he never came home. Mbok followed him to Surabaya and looked for him absolutely everywhere but she never found him.

* Mbok... Please come to Jakarta...

Mak says that Mbok then ran out of money so had to look for a job. While she was looking for a job, Mbok met Ibu Chang, a friend of Mak's. Mbok worked for Ibu Chang and lived with her. Then, when I was born, Ibu Chang invited Mbok round to our house. In the beginning, Mbok would come and help Mak in the mornings and then return to Ibu Chang's house. But one day Mbok properly moved into our house. Mak says that Ibu Chang realised that we needed Mbok at our house even more. And Mbok has lived with us ever since.

'I'll write to you in Tuban, Mbok. OK?'

Suddenly Mbok laughs, even though tears are still down running down her cheeks.

'Don't write me a letter. I can't read, Willa.'

Oh… why can't Mbok read?

I start crying again. Even harder than before.

Mbok hugs me and tells me to be quiet or we'll definitely wake up Mak and Pak.

Mbok is absolutely right.

Mak wakes up and comes into Mbok's room.

She sits down on the edge of the bed.

And the three of us hug.

Leaving

Mak has been busy from first thing this morning.

Pak and Mbok are busy too.

Farida and I wander round the home.

Pak says that Oom Sie is going to pick us up with his car at noon and take us to the airport. It's half past eleven, Mak says. So I'm supposed to eat something so I'm not starving during the journey. Farida's mother brings some steamed sponge cakes for me to have while we're travelling.

Dul (plus walking stick) stands in front of the fence with Bud. They don't say anything. But Bud's eyes dart around and his nose is all wrinkled, what with his nose being full of snot and his being ready to cry. Then two cars drive slowly down the alley and stop in front of our house. Oom Sie and his brother climb out of the two cars. They come straight into the house and begin lifting all the suitcases and boxes that are strapped up and labelled with Pak and Mak's names. Mbok hands me my drinking bottle.

'For the journey.' Then she hugs me tight. I suddenly start crying again. Mbok cries too. Her whole body is shaking.

But before I have time to say anything to Mbok, Mak pulls at my hand.

'Let's go! Come on!'

Mak hugs Mbok, who cries even louder. Me too. Why can't I stay here? I could live with Mbok.

Dul, Bud and Farida are still standing out by the fence. Plus Farida's parents and Gus Salim and Farida's other brothers. Everyone greets Mak and Pak and wishes us safe travels. Farida's mum hugs me. She cries. I cry again.

Before I get in the car, Farida takes my hand. 'You're coming home the day after the day after the day after tomorrow?' she asks.

'Yes, I'll be back the day after the day after the day after tomorrow.'

The car starts moving the moment the doors are shut. Behind us, everyone starts waving furiously. Dul runs beside the car with his stick tucked under his arm, and Bud runs along behind him. But even though he's running as fast as he can, Dul can't catch up with us. The gap between him and the car gets bigger and bigger, but through the car window I can still hear him shouting: 'Willa, write to me! I'll reply! Willa!'

Yes, I'll write to you.

Just don't forget to reply.

Don't forget.

BeSoK - BeSoK - BESoKNYA BeSoK, aku PULANg !!

L 414 NW

* I'll be back the day after the day after
  the day after tomorrow!

Flying

Flying is…

The roar of the car engine, ready to zoom off.

Mak hurries into the car and holds my hand.

Then the car speeds off, turning the corner without slowing. Dul, Ida, Bud and Mbok disappear round the bend.

Flying is…

Having swollen eyes and a runny nose because I've been crying so much.

Mak says I have to stop crying so I don't catch a cold. But how?

But then I start crying again because I remember Very Tiny Yellow Chick had to go to Dul's house.

Flying is…

Queuing then walking up and down stairs and then boarding the plane.

Having to rush because the people behind Mak and Pak are impatient.

They want to sit in their cramped little seats as soon as they can and put their seatbelts over their waists as quickly as possible.

I just want to chat to the lady in the orange uniform with the kind smile.

Flying is...

Feeling the vibrations through your body.

And ringing in your ears.

Your body feeling like it's floating, even though everything around you stays in one place.

And then everything grows smaller and smaller and smaller.

Houses are tiny as matchboxes and then, for a long time, they vanish from view.

Time is like a thread.

Boat and ships are like dots in sparkling blue water.

141

Flying is…

Clouds floating all around the plane.

'I want to touch a cloud, Mak! Can you open the window?' Mak shakes her head.

'You can't open the window because it'd be very dangerous for the plane. Let's just look at the clouds from here.'

But I feel like the cloud is calling me to touch it.

Or it could be somewhere I could play in or jump around on or hide in or lie on.

It must be very soft.

Flying is…

Getting food in a box. With tiny cutlery.

Being called *sweet child* then being given sweets by the lady in the orange uniform.

Then feeling sleepy but waking up again when the plane shakes… then growls… then scrapes along the ground and stops a few moments later.

CLACK CLACK CLACK. Everyone takes off their seatbelts and quickly stands up. They take their bags and boxes and packages down from the lockers overhead. Then they line up, wanting to get off the plane as quick as they can.

Mak grumbles: 'Why is everyone in such a hurry to get off this plane. Don't they realise the plane will wait for us all?'

'Welcome to Jakarta, Willa. You and Mak are going to be very happy here.' Pak smiles, his eyes blinking in the light.

Arriving

After we collect our suitcases and other bags and boxes, they're all pushed and pulled along then heaved into a black car. An old man in a cap helps Pak fit everything into the empty space behind the backseats. Mak tells me this is called the boot of the car.

The old man wearing the cap has a face full of wrinkles. When he smiles, he gets even more wrinkles in the folds of his cheeks and at the corners of his eyes. He holds out his hands which were also wrinkled and covered in moles.

'I'm Pak Kunang.'

'I'm Willa, Pak,' I say.

'Do you want to sit at the front with Pak or behind with Mak?' I turn to Mak. She is standing beside the open car door. Her hair is wild and standing up on end. It's being blown about by the wind in Kemayoran airport.

'Do want to sit at the front? You can,' says Mak.

'Or do you want to sit in front, Mak? I can sit in the back?' asks Pak, opening the front door of the car. Mak shakes her head.

'No need. You two sit in the front, so you get to see the city.' And she gets into the back of the car, sitting in the only bit of free space that's there. Because pretty much the whole backseat is full of the boxes we brought from Surabaya. The car starts to move. Fast.

I sit on Pak's lap.

The sunlight is as sharp as Krembangan Alley. The road is incredibly busy and there are so many people. And bicycles, cars, rickshaws and bemos are all darting about here and there.

My head starts to feel a bit dizzy. Then… in my throat… it's like something wants to pour out. I keeps swallowing, trying to get it to stay inside but this doesn't work. As soon as the car stops, Pak gets out and everything inside me spills out. I've been sick.

'Maybe she has a cold,' says Pak Kunang. Mak massages my neck. Every single thing I ate on the aeroplane has come out. And it does not, I have to say, taste as good this time round. Pak Kunang reaches into his trouser pocket and produces a sweet wrapped in plastic with a picture of a white rabbit on it.

'Try chewing this – to get rid of the horrible taste and stop the nausea,' he says.

From the colour and the picture, this sweet looks decidedly delicious. But it has this sort of thin sticky papery stuff on it. I try and take it off.

'Oh, that's part of it. Just eat it! You don't need to peel it off,' says Pak Kunang, laughing. From where I'm standing, I can see that his teeth are yellow at the front of his mouth and black at the back.

Mak raises her eyebrows and prods the papery bit. Then she grimaces.

'Yep. Pak Kunang's right, Willa. It seems you can eat this paper as well.'

Even though the outside of this rabbit sweet feels like paper, I chew it all the same. I want to get rid of the awful flavour that poured out of me by the car.

And then a little while later... Where are we now? The car has stopped in front of a little house with tall iron railings full of holes. Looking through, I can see there's a big tree right in front of the house's window.

'Is this our house, Mak?'

Pak unlocks the chain that's round the top of the gate. Pak Kunang reverses the car and helps unload everything. Then, picking a key from a big bunch, Pak opens the door to the little house.

Is this our house, Pak?

A different house

'Welcome to Jakarta! This is our new home. Come on!
Come inside, Mak! Willa!' says Pak, bowing to Mak and
me. Mak walks slowly into the house. I follow behind her,
holding onto her skirt.

This house isn't as big or as wide as my house. It's narrow
and long from front to back. At the front of the house is a
sitting room with three low chairs padded with dark yellow
cloth, and a low table. It has two walls across the back. And
in between these two walls is a gap.

'This could be Willa's room,' says Pak. This room-
without-a-door contains a small metal bed with poles that
have a mosquito net tied to them.

'Willa can sleep in here, and her toys can be kept over
here,' says Pak.

The mattress doesn't have any sheets on it.

From here, there's another room which is also connected to
a bathroom.

'This is Mak and Pak's room,' says Pak, squeezing Mak's
shoulder. There's a big metal bed also with poles and a
mosquito net. This mattress doesn't have any sheets on it
either. Then there's a bigger room which connects to the
bathroom.

'We'll make this room into a dining room and a kitchen
at the same time,' says Pak, patting a circular table in the
middle of the room. There are four wooden chairs placed
round it. In the corner of the room is a sink and table made
of cement. Perhaps this is where Mak will do the cooking.

Mak is very quiet.

She looks down at the bottom of the bathroom door which is all uneven, as if it's been nibbled by a mouse. I look at it too. In the bathroom there's a water tank and a toilet. But there's nowhere to have a shower.

'So how is it? This is a nice little house, right? It just needs a lick of paint, a few vases of flowers, some plants…' says Pak, while walking back to the front of the house.

This new house is not like our house in Krembangan Alley. There are no doors to any of the rooms. There are no windows on the side of the house, just a vent with wire mesh on it. And there's nowhere to play on a swing here.

'Where's the pine tree, Pak?'

Pak walks quickly out of the house, and… 'This is your pine tree,' he says, tapping the big tree that stands in front of the window.

So this big tree is a pine tree!

Wow. It is unbelievably tall. This tree looks like it might go all the way to the sky. When I try and hug it, my arms can't reach all the way round it. The trunk is completely straight, without any branches to use as footholds for climbing.

So how am I going to reach the needles to use for my cooking?

And what if Mak wants to make a Christmas tree?

This is not my pine tree.

I want my old pine tree.

'Hey Willa, take a look at this!' Pak is already back in the house, leaning against a long sideboard with three drawers next to one other. Underneath is a little cupboard door, and next to it a wide shelf, without any glass. And underneath *this* is a wooden panel that slides from left to right.

'This is the perfect place to play houses, perhaps,' says Pak. 'Try to get onto this shelf,' he says, pointing at the space. I bend down and climb inside, then lie down on the shelf. Yes yes yes! I absolutely want to make this shelf into a house. I put Teddy Bea and Gorilla on the shelf too.

'Willa – Teddy Bea and Gorilla can't sleep there. And neither can you. We need this sideboard to put books and other things in. It's not for playing houses.' I hear Mak's voice over Pak's shoulder.

Catching a glimpse of Mak's eyebrows, I think maybe I should steer clear of this sideboard.

But when I ask Pak, he winks at me.

Meaning… this shelf could still be a house?

Is that right, Pak?

Tell me straight, Mak and Pak: CAN I PLAY HOUSES HERE OR NOT?

In Jakarta

Elu means you.
Gue means me.
Ape means what.
Iye means yes.
Pegimane means how.
Kenape means why.
Siape means who.
Berape means how much.
Darimane aje means where were you.
Ngapain means what are you doing.
Kagak means no.
Sono means there.
Toge means sprouts.
Kol means rubbish.
Tok-tok-tok means the meatball cart is coming (instead of ting-ting-ting).
Botiiii means bread.
Cuiiii means fish.
Giiiiiing means meat.
Bureeeee means chicken rice porridge.
Bang and Neng mean Cak and Ning.*

Tarik means the bus can start moving again.
Kiri means someone wants the bus to stop.
Asinan means spicy and a little bit sweet. And not salty at

---

* Cak and Ning – traditional costumes worn at festivals and street parades
  (girls' costumes are known as cak, and boys' as ning)

all.

But
Mak is still Mak.
Pak is still Pak.

What're you doing, girl?

NGAPAIN NENG?

KENAPE? Why?

What's that? APE iTu?

BUREEE BERAPE? How much?

ELU DARiMANE?

GUE DARi SoNo! I came from there!

Where do you come from?

SiAPE? Who?

BANG!

Lu KAGAK TAU?

KiRi! Turn left, Bang!

You don't know?

IYE! Yes!

Early days

How long have I been in Jakarta now? How long have I lived in this narrow little house with the enormous pine tree outside and a Dragon water pump and a high gate that creaks every time it's opened and a bed with a mosquito net?

I can't remember now. It certainly feels like a very long time. Every day I think about all the houses in Krembangan Alley and Ida and Dul and Bud and Yellow Chicken and Ibu Juwita and Gatot and Endang…

I just want to go back home to Krembangan Alley.

Pak told me I'd make so many new friends. But I still don't have any friends here. The house to the right of ours is empty. And some people live in the house on the left, but there aren't any children there.

Pak says we'll start looking for a school.

For now though I just hang around inside with Mak while she cleans the house. I really just want to be back at the Juwita Kindergarten with my teacher, Endang, Asih, Sri, Sumi, Eko and Joko.

I've not heard Mak sing for days now. Maybe it's because her records and record player aren't here yet.

Or maybe it's because the little blue and white radio – the replacement for Erres – doesn't play any of Mak's favourite songs.

Whenever Pak turns this blue and white radio on, out comes the voice of a man speaking in English. Mak says this is Pak's favourite radio station. It's called the BBC.

Why not RRI?*

Mak shrugs. 'Maybe Pak doesn't like it.'

But me and Mak love RRI.

All these songs without any singers come out of this radio. They're songs with squeaky high musical instruments instead. Pak says it's called classical music. Then there's also music sung by a man in a very loud voice that shivers and trembles, as though he's got all cold from playing in the rain.

Pak says this is called *opera*.

I really don't like listening to it.

The little blue and white radio lives on top of the sideboard which was so nearly my house. I've never once seen Mak touch the radio but I really want to. Because I want to hear RRI.

Who knows if there are children are singing on the radio?

Who knows if Lilis Suryani or Ernie Djohan are singing too?

Who knows?

---

* RRI – Radio of the Republic of Indonesia

Busy

From the moment we arrived, Mak has been busy sorting out all the things we brought with us from Surabaya. She's also bought some new things for cooking, eating and sleeping.

Mak needs a steamer for cooking rice because there's only one big pot, one small saucepan, three plates, three bowls and six pairs of spoons and forks here. We also need sheets for my bed and for Mak's bed. Plus pillows and pillowcases. Mak also wants to hang a curtain over the gap between the two walls.

Why there isn't just a door?

'For now we're just going to hang some cloth there. We'll get a door someday,' says Mak.

'When is someday, Mak? Is it the day after the day after the day after tomorrow?'

'Something like that. We have to wait until we have enough money. Right now we don't have enough money to buy a door,' says Mak.

Near our house in Jakarta there's place called the Senen Project. We go there in a bemo to try and find all the things we need. It's a bit like Siola, but the size is *something else*. It's like a whole lot of Siolas all stuck together. I think I could easily get lost there if I wasn't with Mak and Pak. Sometimes, if Mak has to buy a lot of things from different places, I hang around waiting for her in Bethlehem Stores on the first floor. This shop is tiny but it's absolutely crammed with stuff.

There are notebooks, picture books, footballs, vests, socks, handkerchiefs, tins of milk powder with pictures of laughing cows on them, corned beef, salty soy sauce in cans with pictures of jumping fish on them, sweet soy sauce with a picture of a stork, and syrup with a white stork surrounded by colourful fruit. I feel just like I used to feel when I'd sit in Cik Mien's shop.

At night, Mak, Pak and I sit out in front of the house under the big pine tree. But we can't stay out for long, as there are always heaps of mosquitoes around. So we then go and sit inside where are no mosquitoes. But boy is it HOT.

'We need a fan,' says Pak, swatting a mosquito away from my head and then his head and then Mak's head.

'Or a mosquito door,' says Mak, batting a mosquito off her foot.

'They'll have to be made specially which will take a while. Let's just buy a fan at Sentosa tomorrow,' says Pak. Sentosa is a shop in the Senen Project that sells just about everything could Mak and Pak need. Spoons, forks, pans… and now fans.

'We also need more air vents with mosquito wire over them. This house really needs more air. But it definitely doesn't need any more mosquitoes,' Mak says.

Pak nods but doesn't say anything.

'There's certainly a lot to do,' says Mak, scratching the mosquito bites on her foot. 'If we hadn't been in such a rush to move, we'd have had time to get all this done beforehand,' Mak continues, swatting a mosquito off her arm. 'We should have got the house sorted out sooner, so we could start looking for a school for Willa… But because we've been so busy with things, she's got so bored.'

Pak doesn't say anything. He keeps smoking.

'When can we go and visit the school you told me about?' asks Mak.

Pak stays quiet.

'Paul, when can we go and look round Willa's school?'

Pak turns to Mak and me.

'I hope the day after tomorrow,' he says.

'The day after tomorrow? You're sure about that? Because I don't want it to be put off again. This child hasn't been to school in almost a month,' says Mak.

Her voice is all high.

I don't like hearing her talk in this voice.

And I don't like seeing Mak's eyebrows all knotted up on her forehead.

And I really don't like hearing her call Pak by his actual name.

Very slowly, I get up from the yellow chair Pak had brought in from the living room.

I go into my doorless bedroom.

I get into bed, climbing inside the mosquito net.

I try and go to sleep.

My eyes are hot.

My nose is runny.

I'm crying.

Is it the day after the day after the day after tomorrow yet?

The tape

In our new house, the blue and white radio starts playing the moment Pak wakes up. A man and a woman speak in English. And all the songs are in English. As soon as Pak leaves the house, Mak turns the radio off. It seems Mak isn't all that keen on the blue and white radio. Maybe she misses her records that haven't arrived from Surabaya yet. I heard Mak ask Pak when her records will get here. Pak said 'next week'. Then when next week arrived, Pak said 'next week' again.

'It seems Oom Sie's been busy so he hasn't had time to send them to Jakarta yet.'

Perhaps.

This afternoon Pak gets home from work earlier than usual. He's carrying a big cloth bag with a big box in it which he puts on the sideboard.

'What is it, Pak?'

'It's a present for Mak!' he says, opening the big brown box that says TOSHIBA on it. Mak watches Pak as he takes out what looks like a metal box. It has a wire coming out of it that connects to the electricity. Pak presses some buttons on the box and a little door opens. Inside there are two small wheels.

'Mak, this is a tape recorder. It plays tapes of songs. Tapes are like records, but they're smaller and easier to use. And if you want to take this tape player somewhere, you can put batteries in it. Why don't you have a go with it?'

Then Pak takes out some small plastic rectangular boxes.

Each one has a picture on the front and inside it is another little plastic rectangular box with two holes that have cogs inside.

'This is a tape. It holds lots of songs – even more than on a record. So, you put it in the machine like this… press 'play'… and then listen… Sounds good, yes?,' says Pak.

Pak's right. Each tape holds so many songs. And once you've finished one side of a tape, you turn it over and it plays even more songs. Pak can sing along with just about every song on these tapes. Perhaps these are Pak's favourite songs.

They aren't songs that Mak knows. But there's one song I really like. It's sung by a grey-haired woman in a voice that sounds like she has a particularly nasty cold. Pak says the woman is French. On the cover, it says her name is Françoise Hardy.

Bored

I still haven't started school.

While I wait, I've just been staying at home (of course) with Mak.

I do the same-old same-old things: playing with the Dragon pump that spurts water if you fill it up at the top with a bucket; gathering fallen pine needles into little piles, listening to Pak's tapes and to the blue and white radio. But I'm bored of doing all this. I only want one thing: school.

But the school that Pak mentioned – Gunung Sahari Elementary School – only starts in January. And right now it's July. So I have to wait.

I'm so bored of waiting.

Postcards

Pak brought me a postcard this afternoon.

'It shows Monas, which is the National Monument in Jakarta. You should send it to Dul, Willa. You promised you'd write him a letter, right?' says Pak.

A ha, yes!

On the back of this picture of the monument (that I'd already seen in Dul's geography textbook) is where I should write to Dul.

'But what should I write, Pak?'

'Tell him about all the things you've seen here, what you've been doing… Anything. Dul will want to know all about everything.'

OK, I'll do that.

I'm going to tell him that my house is near to the Senen Project, which is much bigger than Siola.

And my house is no longer down an alley, but on a wide and busy street.

Over the road, there's a big wall and behind this wall are railway tracks, just like at the end of Krembangan Alley.

There's a pine tree that reaches as high as the sky, but I'm already bored playing cooking with its leaves which are thin and sharp as needles.

In our house we have a tape recorder and cassettes which play lots of different songs.

And we don't have a well with a borehole at our house. Instead we have a tall metal Dragon pump next to the pine tree. To get water to come out, you first have to fill up one of its nostrils with some water.

Hey, and how's Yellow Chicken doing at your house?

Dear Dul,

I start writing.

But then I stop.

I just want to be able to sit next to him and tell him everything. Maybe while we wind up some kite string together.

I don't want to send him a postcard.

I want to go home.

About the author

Reda Gaudiamo is a writer from Jakarta, Indonesia. She was born in 1962 and wrote her first story when she was in the first grade, reading it to her parents after dinner time. She first had her work published while studying French literature in the University of Indonesia. Later she had her work published by national newspapers and magazines.

Her first book – *Bisik-bisik / Whispers*, a short story collection consisting of dialogues – was published in 2004. Since then, she has published three more short story collections: *Pengantin Baru / Newly-Weds* (2010), *Tentang Kita / About Us* (2015) and *Potret Keluarga / Family Portrait* (2021).

In 2012, she published her first children's book: *Na Willa*. This was followed by *Meps, Beps and Me* (2016) – a collaboration with her daughter Soca Sobhita – and *Na Willa and the House in the Alley* (2018). These last two books were published by Post Press, who also reprinted *Na Willa*. In August 2022, the third book in the Na Willa series – *Na Willa dan Hari-hari Ramai / Na Willa and the Busy Days* – was released. In February 2023, she published her new book *Hai Nak!* which is dedicated to her 390K followers on TikTok.

Reda is also well known as a singer and musician through the AriReda duo, whose poetry-inspired ballads have captivated audiences across Southeast Asia and Europe. In October 2022 she launched her self-titled solo album, *Reda Gaudiamo*, which she wrote her own lyrics and music. You can find her on Spotify.

Instagram: @reda.gaudiamo
Twitter: @RedaGaudiamo

About the illustrator

Cecillia Hidayat is an INFJ who speaks her mind best through her drawings.

She spent four years working in advertising agencies before deciding that she's too old at heart for all the big city hustle and bustle.

She was born in Jakarta and now lives in Ubud with her husband. She spends most of her days drawing, walking between ricefields while petting the stray dogs she meets along the way, and watching the 'Cooking With Dog' YouTube channel religiously.

Instagram: @inicecil

About the translators

Ikhda Ayuning Maharsi Degoul is a Javanese Indonesian-born French poet, creative director, independent curator, and art teacher currently living in Canada. Her debut poetry pamphlet, *Ikhda, by Ikhda*, was published by the Emma Press in 2014. Her poems have been published in *The Emma Press Anthology of Mildly Erotic Verse* and *The Emma Press Anthology of Motherhood*. Her second poetry collection, *The Goldfish*, was published as an illustrated art book by the Emma Press in 2019.

Instagram: @ikhdadegoul

Kate Wakeling is a poet and musicologist. Her debut poetry collection for children, *Moon Juice*, won the CLiPPA in 2017 and was nominated for the Carnegie Medal. Her second collection, *Cloud Soup*, was shortlisted for the CLiPPA in 2022 and named a book of the month in the *Guardian* and the *Scotsman*.

A pamphlet of Kate's poetry for adults, *The Rainbow Faults*, is published by The Rialto. Kate studied music at Cambridge University and holds a PhD in Balinese gamelan music from SOAS.

Website: katewakeling.co.uk
Twitter: @WakelingKate
Instagram: @kate_wakeling

Ideas for your own stories, poems and pictures

Now it's your turn to make some stories, poems and pictures! Here are some ideas to get you started...

◆

Have you ever moved house? It's a very big deal, whatever age you are, and it can come with complicated feelings. You might be excited about your new home, but you might miss things about your old home too. **Write a letter to your old home**, telling it what your new home is like.

◆

Willa promises Farida that she will come back and visit 'the day after the day after the day after tomorrow'. Write a list of all the most amazing things you would like to happen in the future and then **write a story called 'The Day after the Day after the Day after Tomorrow'**, where all of them happen... all on the same day!

◆

Pak is always doodling. Let's have a go at that ourselves... Take pen and a blank piece of paper or a page in a notebook, sit next to a window, and fill the page with doodles. **Put the pen to the paper and doodle away!** Don't worry about making things perfect – just let your thoughts drift and see where they take you. You could doodle things that you see around you or out of the window, or things that pop into your brain. When you've filled your page, take a step back and admire your work!

When Farida has chickenpox, Willa can't play with her and she gets incredibly bored and frustrated. Think about what makes you frustrated and reasons you get bored, and write them all down. Then **write a poem titled 'I'm Bored!'**.

Willa is so excited about her auntie Lan coming to visit! She tries to find out as much about her as possible before she comes. **Think of one of your favourite people in the world** and do some writing about them. Describe what they are like and some of your favourite memories of them. Maybe you can show it them when you've finished...?

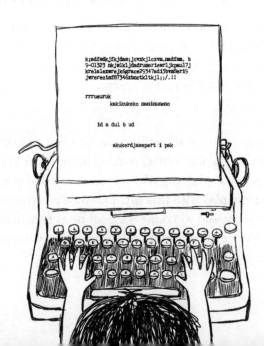

Be an illustrator! Not all of the stories in this book have an illustration to go with them, so **pick a story without a picture and draw an illustration for it**. If there's space on the page (and this isn't a library book), you could even do it directly into the book! Think about important moments in the story and images come into your head when you think about it – this could give you inspiration for how to illustrate the story.

Do you speak languages other than English? **Think about your favourite words in a different language and write a list poem** like on page 149 ('In Jakarta'). You might like these words because of their sounds or because of their meanings, or because of memories associated with them. Remember: they don't need to rhyme! But if you like, you could put the words in an order that tells a kind of story.

If you don't speak any other languages, now's the time to start! Find a foreign language dictionary in the library and look up some of your favourite words in English, and see what they are in a different language.

Have you got a toy or something else that you reaaaally don't like sharing, like Willa's rocking horse Poni? **Write a short speech explaining why it is essential that you and you alone can play with this toy**. Everyone is trying to make you share and you don't want to! Be as persuasive as possible – you can even make things up, about what might happen if you are forced to share!

ABOUT THE EMMA PRESS

small press, big dreams

☙❧

The Emma Press is an independent publishing house based in the Jewellery Quarter, Birmingham, UK. It was founded in 2012 by Emma Dai'an Wright and specialises in poetry, short fiction and children's books.

In 2020 The Emma Press received funding from Arts Council England's Elevate programme, developed to enhance the diversity of the arts and cultural sector by strengthening the resilience of diverse-led organisations.

The Emma Press is passionate about publishing literature which is welcoming and accessible.

Visit our website and find out more about our books here:

Website: theemmapress.com
Facebook @theemmapress
Twitter @theemmapress
Instagram @theemmapress